British Welfare Policy: Workhouse to Workfare

Anne Digby is a Senior Lecturer in Social History at Oxford Polytechnic. She is the author of several books on the history of social policy and the social history of medicine including *Pauper Palaces* (1978) and *Madness, Morality and Medicine* (1985).

D0300373

BRITISH WELFARE POLICY: WORKHOUSE TO WORKFARE

Anne Digby

faber and faber

LONDON · BOSTON

First published in 1989
by Faber and Faber Limited
3 Queen Square London WCIN 3AU

Typeset by Wilmaset, Birkenhead, Wirral
Printed in Great Britain by
Richard Clay Ltd, Bungay, Suffolk

*British Library Cataloguing in Publication Data
is available*

ISBN 0-571-14663-5

Series Editors
Avner Offer – University of York
F. M. L. Thompson – Institute of Historical Research,
University of London

It is widely recognized that many of the problems of present-day society are deeply rooted in the past, but the actual lines of historical development are often known only to a few specialists, while the policy-makers and analysts themselves frequently rely on a simplified, dramatized, and misleading version of history. Just as the urban landscape of today was largely built in a world that is no longer familiar, so the policy landscape is shaped by attitudes and institutions formed under very different conditions in the past. This series of specially commissioned handbooks aims to provide short, up-to-date studies in the evolution of current problems, not in the form of narratives but as critical accounts of the ways in which the present is formed by the past, and of the roots of present discontents. Designed for those with little time for extensive reading in the specialized literature, the books contain full bibliographies for further study. The authors aim to be as accurate and comprehensive as possible, but not anodyne; their arguments, forcefully expressed, make the historical experience available in challenging form, but do not presume to offer ready-made solutions.

Contents

List of Tables and Figures

Preface

I was born in the year of the Beveridge Report – a veritable child of the classic welfare state – and achieved adulthood in the sixties – a decade of unequalled optimism about the potential of state welfare. This personal history has meant that it has been particularly stimulating to write a history of welfare from the perspective of the restrictionist eighties. The need for such a volume became obvious while teaching courses at the University of York. I have tried to fill a gap in the literature between historical accounts of welfare usually ending with Beveridge, and social policy publications focusing on the very recent past.

The incisive comments of the editors, Avner Offer and Michael Thompson, have helped to clarify the analysis, while their patience in waiting for the completion of the manuscript has been exemplary. Conversation with many friends and colleagues has been helpful in challenging and refining my ideas. The perceptive criticisms of the text made by Jane Lewis have been particularly useful. And Charles Feinstein's contribution to the author's intellectual and personal welfare has been invaluable.

Researching and writing the book on both sides of the Atlantic has contributed both to its shape and title. It has also facilitated the use of some superb libraries. I should like to thank the librarians of the Widener Library at Harvard University and the Green Library at Stanford University, as well as those at Nuffield College, and the Institute of Economics and Statistics, in the University of Oxford.

I

Introduction

This book aims to place current debate on British welfare provision more firmly within the context of the historical development of social policy, since much discussion (both political and specialist) has very short time horizons. The lesson of history is that it does not repeat itself precisely, yet, on a broader front, certain policy issues, dilemmas, problems and choices do recur in social welfare. To forget the past record of these events is to force each generation to relearn what should already be known, and thus make future developments less satisfactory than they might be. Equally undesirable, however, has been the tendency in some quarters to manufacture a fictitious past; to create a past golden age of mythical virtues which present policy can seek to emulate. Through each of these ahistorical tendencies, current debate on social welfare is made less informed and cogent.

That British concern over the welfare state had reached unprecedented heights was shown by the 1987 general election which, for the first time, placed 'social' rather than 'economic' issues at the centre of the campaign. Earlier, in the mid-twentieth century, the incrementalist character of social welfare had made it a secondary electoral issue. It was then a matter of alternative 'shopping lists' between contending parties, whose rival programmes were concerned with the exact configurations of welfare topography rather than with the actual existence of the welfare state itself. 'Rolling back the frontiers' of the welfare state, the battle-cry of the New Right from the mid-seventies onwards, reopened more fundamental questions of collectivism versus individualism – of social as against individual responsibility – that had not been major issues for discussion since the early years of the century. The legitimacy of welfare statism was placed on the central political agenda by politicians and commentators whose ideas had previously seemed anachronistic and unrealistic. That they were enabled to do so was the product of a number of interrelated factors.

The dependence of social welfare on the availability of economic resources was an inconvenient truism that it was all too easy for Britons to overlook in decades of economic growth – the fifties and sixties. Those years marked the highest period of sustained growth experienced in modern British economic history.[1] The golden age of 'Beveridge's' welfare state appeared then to go hand in hand with 'Keynes's' *managed* economy. In reality, the government's role in the creation and control of this buoyant economy was limited since the maintenance of a full employment policy (which *inter alia* reduced the amount needed for social security payments) was mainly the product of non-governmental factors. The engine of growth was driven both by rapid capital formation (arising from a lengthy backlog of investment opportunities), and by expanding exports resulting from unusually favourable world trading conditions. But by the seventies, economic growth had faltered under inflationary pressures, a wage spiral that owed much to British trade union power in conditions of full employment, and a more general price rise precipitated by OPEC's oil hike in 1973. In the late seventies and early eighties an intensifying international recession, with unemployment rates that in some cases – as in Britain – rivalled those of the inter-war depression, focused international attention on the relationship between the economic and social policies of governments. Concern grew that finite resources were underpinning welfare policies with a social dynamic of their own. A 'fiscal crisis' was discerned, whereby continued growth in welfare provision might itself undermine the economic base for its own future. In a period of stagflation (where there was inflation, slow economic growth and unemployment) there was an increasing awareness that social policy might produce unwanted side-effects on economic efficiency. High marginal tax rates could discourage wealth creation, and work incentives be harmed by the allegedly small margin between the fruits of labour and those of welfare. Rising citizen expectations of social policy, together with worsening dependency ratios as a result of an ageing population, served only to heighten the urgency of tackling the welfare issue on the political agenda.

Politicians were encouraged in this task in the late seventies by a 'welfare backlash' of international proportions. In Britain the Conservative party, under Mrs Thatcher, won power in 1979 with promises to cut taxes and reduce bureaucracy in order to enhance individual liberty and self-reliance rather than dependence on the welfare state. An era of financial constraint appeared to have made many voters more conscious of their purse-strings than their heartstrings; costs achieved higher public visibility than benefits. However, support for certain social policies continued; voters wanted both lower taxes *and* the maintenance of the 'core' welfare services of pensions, education and the National Health Service. This more selective support for the welfare state was a world-wide phenomenon; societies divided between the employed and the unemployed – the 'them' and the 'us' – of those in work or on welfare. Media and public attention targeted welfare 'chisellers' in the USA, 'dolebludgers' in Australia or 'scroungers' in Britain. Those adopting such attitudes might be expected to give electoral support for the adoption of more restrictionist social policies, in which the consequences of austerity fell disproportionately on the poor. By the early eighties there was some disillusionment in Britain over the ability of the state to realize the extensive social goals that had been added to the more limited objectives of Beveridge's classic welfare state of the forties. Loss of confidence in the power of government to deliver full employment went hand in hand with declining faith in the power of the welfare bureaucracy to deliver adequate – or even disinterested – service.

This more critical attitude was a product of several factors. Antibureaucratic sentiment was expressed both from the political right and from the left; while the former stressed its wastefulness, the latter deprecated its remoteness and inhumanity, although each (for differing reasons) disliked the dependent helplessness to which welfare administration might reduce its clients. And the conclusions of social policy analysts on the creation of 'diswelfare' meant that there was a growing – if rather nebulous – public awareness that the actual results of welfare legislation and regulation could differ from those that had been intended. An uneasy recognition that each change in social security regulations might create a new anomaly was fostered by the predominantly right-wing press which made a human-interest story out of individuals who suffered as a result of the changes. The intrinsically expansive nature of the welfare state and the relativism of 'cultural poverty' also contributed to a more hostile climate of opinion, since it meant that 'we constantly manufacture new forms of poverty as we drive forward the living standards of the majority'.[2] Paradoxically, this seemed to have produced contradictory responses: popular feeling – intensified by the media – was directed both against those who were seen to have done well out of welfare benefits (since the standard of supplementary benefits went up broadly in line with general living standards), *and* against those who, through anomalies, had done badly. In addition, the hidden costs of welfare that earlier had been discussed in specialist, but little-read, publications now attracted a wider audience since, in an era of financial constraint, the distorting effects of 'welfare constituencies' on the distribution of resources were more readily apparent. The right-wing views of the Institute of Economic Affairs, which earlier had appeared of relevance only to a few neo-conservatives, now attracted more widespread attention. In particular, Seldon's view that the welfare state had 'turned from an engine of mercy to an instrument and producer of vested interests'[3] seemed particularly relevant when public service unions defended the status quo against the projected cuts of democratically elected governments. The 'winter of discontent' of 1978–9 acted as a catalyst in a hardening of public attitudes on this issue.

Margaret Thatcher's electoral victory in 1979 has usually been taken to mark the beginning of a new era of anti-collectivism, and one that was packaged attractively to the electorate with 'Victorian' values of individual liberty, self-reliance and reward for effort. Old arguments, last aired comprehensively in Edwardian days, were revived within the context of a new ideological environment manufactured by the New Right.[4] Britain was to enter a period of renewed economic growth based on tax cuts, elimination of bureaucratic 'waste' and the reassertion of work incentives, achieved in part through welfare reforms. This Thatcherite watershed concealed some underlying continuities; until the legislation of 1987–8, rhetoric was more striking than reform in welfare. During this interim period a shift in popular values which would support such legislative change gradually became apparent in an appreciation both of the value of market mechanisms to achieve efficiency and of the desirability of greater individual choice. Approval for a mixed economy of public and private welfare, but with a redrawn boundary between the two constituents, has been the most important consequence of these changing values. While not going to the extremes of privatization and voluntaryism present in Reaganite America, the Conservative administration in Britain has encouraged a more restrictive welfare role for public bodies and an enhanced role for private ones. A new emphasis has been placed on the state as facilitator rather than as provider, with encouragement for private action through exhortation, guidelines, legislation or incentives. Hayek's 'road to serfdom' appears to be no longer in such good repair. Instead, Britons are effectively being asked to ponder the wisdom of Peacock's earlier dictum: 'the true object of the Welfare State is to teach people how to do without it'.[5]

Choice for the individual has been the central piece of rhetoric in the attempt since 1979 to beat back public welfare. The New Right has presented itself as the champion of a property-owning democracy where small capitalists are freed from the oppressive restrictions of socialistic welfare. Thatcher's authoritarian populism had made its appeal to national rather than class interests. It has been designed to operate through the activity of a neutral market place which is depicted as operating in the interests of all citizens instead of the sectional interests involved in state welfare.[6] The Prime Minister has been seen as a populist Conservative in the nineteenth-century tradition of figures like Disraeli, yet her policies are much more authoritarian than those of her predecessors. A *partnership* between central and local government was a crucial element in earlier policies whereas, during the eighties, the heavy hand of central government has been particularly obvious in crushing local government autonomy. What has been termed the Thatcherite revolution has not involved merely a simple replacement of collectivism by individualism, but instead has reshuffled the respective spheres of local and central, or public and private. Welfare changes in the eighties have involved a centralist thrust in their reassertion of individual responsibilities. In this respect there is a certain symmetry between the eighties and Beveridge's earlier revolution. In the creation of the classic welfare state of the 1940s, expanded frontiers of public welfare concealed an underlying assertion of the necessity for personal responsibility in determining a destiny beyond that minimum standard ensured by collectivist action.

Historically, the role of personal responsibility in relation to welfare benefits has been the subject of more or less continuous debate during the last two centuries. The creation of a national workhouse system after 1834 was designed to reassert the importance of individual effort by fit adults, and to cut back on what was seen as over-generous public provision of welfare benefits to them. The more recent debate on workfare (where benefits are given in return for work) has had the same rationale. Interestingly, in both cases – workhouse and workfare – the terms have become a kind of shorthand for a much wider set of assumptions, attitudes and policies linking social welfare to the efficient operation of the economy. This has influenced the wording of the title of this book in its discussion of continuity and change in welfare policies. From the perspective of the right both workhouse and workfare systems have been justified in relation to a reassertion of work-incentives through a lower benefit/wage ratio that aimed to cut the numbers of those who 'chose' welfare rather than work. From the left, the workhouse system came to symbolize a poor-law philosophy that led to an unacceptable degree of compulsion, conditionality of benefits, and stigma. Even after the legal end of the Poor Law in 1948, its shadow fell over those who designed the new system in which welfare benefits were to be given as of right to the citizen. It was therefore to be expected that the adoption of workfare during the eighties – whether 'old-style' compulsory schemes or 'new-style' voluntary ones – has been seen by the political left as a return to the older system of welfare. One MP, during a recent debate on the new government employment policies – the Youth Training Scheme and the Employment Training Scheme – articulated these fears when he stated, 'We are returning to a Poor Law philosophy on the back of workfare.'[7]

A study of the long-term evolution of British welfare policy suggests that it involves the adoption or rejection of competing ideas. These include economic as well as social issues since, for example, the impact of social welfare programmes on economic efficiency has been a recurrent object of concern. This book is concerned primarily with the 'how' and the 'why' of changes in the social policies of the past. However, welfare policies are not merely technical but also ideological; the difficulty of separating the empirical from the normative has meant that the discussion may also involve issues of what 'ought' to be in social policy. Surveying the varied limits of collective responsibility for individual contingencies in the history of social policy throws some light on what might be termed the ethical foundations of welfare. Recent discussion on developments in the welfare state has highlighted the competing claims of efficiency and equity and suggested alternative principles of social justice. The egalitarianism that informed the post-war consensus on social welfare has been challenged. Influential in this context has been John Rawl's *A Theory of Justice* (1971). Here a discussion of the problem of trade-off between equality and efficiency led to the conclusion that inequality was permissible if it enhanced the welfare of those who were worst advantaged.[8]

The historical development of British public welfare policy from the workhouse of the 1830s to the workfare schemes of the 1980s is analysed in Chapters III, IV, V and VII. Chapter III includes analyses of the first two of the three subperiods between the 1830s and the 1980s when state intervention in social policy notably increased. It focuses first on the creation of the workhouse system in the 1830s, before examining Victorian dilemmas over the respective areas of individual and collective responsibility, and the relevance these debates had for the formation of the Edwardian social service state in the early twentieth century. The complex transition from that social service state of limited welfare services for the poor to the optimal and universal ones of the classic welfare state of the forties[9] (the third subperiod when state intervention grew significantly), is the subject of Chapter IV. Chapter V discusses the continuities and discontinuities in welfare policies that followed during the next four decades; continuity in the limited bipartisan support for core welfare services, and discontinuity in that the optimism and expansionism of the fifties and sixties was succeeded by the more restrictive approach of the seventies and early eighties. Chapter VII focuses on the impact of neo-liberal thought on the redrawing of boundaries between individualism and collectivism and its results in the social policies of the third Thatcher administration. Their radical nature, it is argued, constitutes a decisive change in welfare provision comparable to those of the 1830s, 1900s and 1940s. In important respects these very recent changes in policy have come full circle in relation to the earliest policies of *public* welfare discussed in this book, since workfare and workhouse arose from similar concerns and draw on the same individualistic philosophy. Chapter VI is concerned with the parallel, long-term development of *private* welfare from the Victorian period onwards. It includes brief surveys of voluntaryism, informal welfare in the family and community, and fiscal and occupational welfare. This picture of the highly divisible nature of welfare that has grown up in Britain is complemented by material in Chapter II which suggests that welfare predicaments are in some sense indivisible so that it is also relevant to examine international developments. In order fully to understand our own welfare policies in the present, we must take into account not only time but space – past policies in Britain and recent ones in other advanced capitalist countries. It is to the latter that we now turn.

II

Comparative Perspectives

Uncertainties about the future of the welfare state were given an international focus in 1980 by a conference organized by the Organization for Economic Cooperation and Development (OECD). Entitled 'The Welfare State in Crisis', it explored the implications of the current clash between economic and social policies.[1] The 'economic crisis', as it was then perceived, involved a combination of slower economic growth rates, inflation and unemployment in the twenty-four member countries. With obstinately high public expenditures, of which welfare spending formed a major part, attention was given to ways of containing the expansionist tendencies of social welfare. The principle of efficiency as against equity and the application of this, in terms of selective or universal welfare benefits, was central to the discussions. The implications of the 'burden' of public expenditures for the market economy received more intermittent attention, and concern was expressed over the erosion of work-incentives and of rigidities in the labour market, as a result of advanced welfare programmes. A more recent OECD report has looked at patterns of expenditure since 1960.[2] We will return to its analysis at the end of this chapter. Before we do, it seems important to look back at the process which has led to this expansion of welfare, since the origins of these programmes occurred more than a century ago in Britain and other developed capitalist countries.

Such a comparative view of welfare is preferable to that ethnocentric perspective (all too common in discussions of social policy) which tends to overemphasize the singularity of the issues within a single country – usually one's own. It has additional value in bringing about a better understanding of the different options that are available in social policy and thus helps to replace the traditionally narrow view in Britain in which the state is seen as the main provider of welfare benefits. With an increasing trend towards mixed systems of welfare in many countries – including Britain – it is particularly relevant today to see how different societies have responded to social need.[3] This is not to argue in favour of welfare convergence as an explanation for similar developments in policy. While it is possible to see cross-influences in social policy, or even borrowing of ideas, the social, cultural and economic circumstances of individual states have typically produced distinctive strategies. Parallel development rather than convergence is a more apt description of this process of evolution.[4] But this needs to be qualified by the recognition that while there are broad similarities in general problems, welfare responses are usually differentiated.

It is possible to interpret the welfare state's emergence in several different ways. First, there is a "push" theory of *demand*-driven development. Here, welfare states are seen as emerging in a few developed countries during the closing decades of the nineteenth century as a response to industrialization and urbanization. This kind of economically determined analysis has been supplemented by those which emphasize the importance of the extension of the suffrage and the political mobilization of the working class. Second, the *supply* or 'pull' theories of the origin of welfare states emphasize the importance of market forces in determining the correct supply of social services. A third type of explanation places emphasis on the relationship between social change and the *state*, where the state is seen as an autonomous actor which searches and experiments in social-policy making.[5]

The attractions of the demand-led theories are strong although they may pay insufficient attention to the complexities of varied institutional structures and governmental response. For example, the development of social welfare as a response to industrial development took varied forms: Germany pioneered a compulsory, national system of contributory health insurance in 1884; in France considerable resistance to the expansion of state involvement in welfare meant that voluntary and municipal provision remained important; and in Britain the older mechanisms of a statutory Poor Law combined with voluntary charitable provision began to be supplemented both with employers' schemes and social insurance by the early twentieth century. It is also notable that some of the earliest welfare provision was not related to industrial development since it was wealthy Denmark – predominantly rural and agricultural – that first introduced (non-contributory) old-age pensions in 1891, an example followed shortly afterwards by a similarly agrarian country – New Zealand. Reasons for the expansion of welfare provision at this time were in fact diverse, frequently featuring not only economic factors but social and political issues as well. Prominent amongst them were arguments about national efficiency and eugenics. In this context it is interesting to note Rimlinger's explanation for the origins of social security in many countries, as constituting a 'Liberal Break' with a traditional repressive paternalism that was seen as increasingly in conflict with the economic and social needs of modern industrial states.[6] The importance of a political dimension was obvious in the plans by the New Liberalism for social insurance. These were opposed by the political right as a violation of individual responsibility, and by the left (in the form of organized labour) as insufficiently egalitarian or socialistic. The attitude of organized labour movements to state welfare was therefore ambivalent while modern industrial capital showed considerable interest in promoting welfare improvements. In general, however, it is important to appreciate that these early incursions into social policy were of an experimental nature and were also very selective: by the early twentieth century, advances had been made mainly in educational provision for the young, pensions for some of the old, and in restricted schemes for sickness insurance and workers' accident compensation.

The period from the First World War to the seventies was one of consolidation and extension in the evolution of welfare states, but the differential impact of inter-war depression and of war produced divergent rates of change. War, involving mass participation in the struggle, was a catalyst for more widespread welfare benefits. Citizens' expectations were raised by wartime experiences; war had been fought not only *against* the enemy but *for* a better peacetime future. In the twenties such aspirations tended to be blunted in several countries by the need for financial retrenchment. However, the even more depressed years of the thirties did force some notable extensions in social policy, as in the New Deal in the USA. This gave this 'welfare laggard' better provision than in European countries, such as France or Italy, which had begun it earlier. In the Second World War the need to mobilize civilians as well as soldiers, together with an even greater involvement of the state in social and economic life, led to improved welfare benefits in Britain and, to a lesser extent, in Australia and New Zealand. And, for those European countries which had suffered occupation, the pressing need for post-war restructuring, and a desire to strengthen political stability through improved welfare provision, contributed to an extension of social benefits in Norway, Holland, Belgium, Austria and France. Typically, these later social policy developments were in the fields of family allowances or child and maternity benefits, in improved pensions, and in extended health and unemployment insurance

The form and extent of welfare should also be seen in relation to political ideology; a free market approach (as in the USA or Canada) has resulted in a more limited public role than in countries where there is extensive but centralized provision (as in Scandinavia). In its mixture of state and voluntary agencies and its moderate level of provision, Britain would have a middle ranking here. To illustrate these divergences and situations we shall look briefly at the historical experience of the USA, as a reluctant welfare state, and Sweden as an advanced welfare state, in relation to that of Britain – discussed at length later in the volume.

Sweden and the USA: Welfare and Workfare

The welfare state in Sweden is universalist and egalitarian in that it seeks to provide for the whole population rather than to target resources on groups with special needs. Welfare is intended to integrate rather than to divide the members of society. Social citizenship confers upon Swedes a wide range of welfare entitlements which are designed to provide the decent (rather than the minimum) standard of living that is considered appropriate to an advanced democracy. One example of the more extended range of benefits to which this philosophy leads is the provision for housewives (a neglected species in most welfare states) to take annual vacations. The development of this comprehensive and integrated structure had been helped by the dominance between 1932 and 1976 of the Social Democrats in Swedish politics, and their support by a highly organized labour movement. In the thirties the Social Democrats introduced child and maternity benefits, and unemployment insurance, and also improved a system of pensions that had been started in 1913. Family allowances, housing subsidies, widow's and orphan's pensions, health insurance, and a statutory three weeks' annual holiday followed in the years after the war. By the sixties the range of benefits was so comprehensive that the Minister of Social Affairs commented, 'The purpose of the general reforms . . . [has been] to give everyone security . . . Now . . . we must move towards individual neglected groups. This is the last brick in our edifice.'[7] As a result, social workers sought out clients, giving aid before citizens sought it, in an attempt to provide preventative rather than curative help.

It would be misleading to see the Swedish welfare system as similar to the British in focusing social welfare mainly in terms of cash benefits. Instead the Swedes have relied on labour market policies as a major means of achieving social goals. Rather than provide cash assistance to the unemployed, temporary jobs or training have been made available through large-scale programmes. A workfare element is important in the Swedish system since benefits are made conditional on readiness to accept work or participate in training. The Swedish Employment Service has long had an integrated function whereby it both monitors cash disbursements to the unemployed and evaluates the individual's need for training or job placement. The service ensures that the adult unemployed receive benefits only after meeting the condition that they are actively seeking work; benefit is refused after a claimant refuses a job or training offer twice. This offer may not be a local one since there is an expectation that the unemployed may need to move to another region in order to take up a job. For the young an even stronger element of workfare is apparent in the training and employment schemes operated for those under twenty who have left school but not found a job. No cash benefits on their own are available to this age group; benefits are gained solely as a result of participation in a training or relief work programme. Within three weeks of registration at an Employment Service Office, an eighteen or nineteen year old must be placed in the youth workfare system. And for the few under-eighteens who have left school, the Employment Service must cooperate with the school to find placements in special programmes of youth jobs.[8] Sweden's corporatist tradition – with centralized channels for negotiation between the state, labour and management – has facilitated an efficient operation of workfare and the acceptance by the labour movement of its merits.

Welfare policies in Sweden have contributed to substantial improvements in living standards. The number of people experiencing multiple deprivation has declined. But, despite this, welfare problems still remain unevenly distributed in society. Predictably, lack of economic resources has been associated with a high risk of problem states such as poor housing or ill-health. The vulnerable groups are women, the aged, and the working class. A widening of the gap between the incomes of the bulk of the population and the minority at the base of society has been conspicuous. Sweden's class three – the working class – are falling behind in income, while class two move closer to class one; equalization of earned and disposable income has not continued into the eighties.[9]

The advanced nature of the Swedish welfare state has not made it immune to criticism; rather the reverse. Feminists have acknowledged the benefits of a high level of public services – such as childcare facilities or care for the elderly – in facilitating women's integration into the labour market. But they have deprecated the minimal role of women in decision-making in public welfare systems. They have argued that women's private dependence (in the family) has been exchanged only for a public dependence (on the state), so that patriarchy has persisted, although its form has altered.[10] The Swedish welfare state, as an 'attempt to synthesize capitalism and socialism'[11], has predictably been criticized from both the political right and from the left, and with an interesting convergence in assertion. Marxists have alleged that its 'reformism' has merely buttressed capitalism; it has created working-class dependency and passivity while leaving the social structure and economy untouched. From the radical right the all-caring society has been criticized for developing social-security servitude and dependency on the state.[12] And the international economic recession in the seventies led to right-wing demands that 'spending must be adjusted to the economic resources available if the economy is not to suffer'.[13] This was linked to criticism of the way in which the corporatist structure had created a welfare 'demand-machine' that was hard to resist. As a result the strongly redistributive social policies pursued were alleged to be destroying the very forces that had created prosperity, both through over-high taxes to finance large public-sector expenditures, and an inflexible labour market that resulted from full-employment policies.[14]

How valid are such criticisms? There have been allegations from both left and right that the Swedish welfare system leads to passivity, isolation and lack of initative. This is not supported by contemporary evidence in such social indicators as mental well-being, frequency of family contacts, and participation in educational or political activities. All suggest that the Swedish welfare system has raised, not lowered, its citizens' aspirations and activities.[15] And turning from social to economic life, with an unemployment rate that has not exceeded 3.5 per cent, the Swedish experience of full employment can give small comfort to those who associate 'welfare dependency' with a sluggish labour market. During the eighties there has been an increase in the hours worked as part-time work declined and absences from work also fell. Nor, despite the fact that tax rates as a percentage of gross domestic product had risen from 28.5 to 52.2 between 1960 and 1986, does Swedish prosperity give much comfort to those who believe that high levels of state expenditure were inimical to economic progress. Per capita income levels in Sweden are exceeded only by those of Switzerland, Japan and the USA.[16]

The USA, like Sweden, was a late starter in developing a welfare state. But, unlike Sweden, an emphasis on self-reliance and rugged individualism provided a cold ideological climate for the creation of public welfare. Historically, poverty was generally seen as deriving from individual fault, so that welfare policy was consequently punitive and aimed both to deter the poor from seeking relief and to instil social discipline. This perpetuated a minimalist policy of poor relief well into the twentieth century. The dominant image of the poor remained a degraded one, with only a minority of 'worthy' poor deemed suitable objects for assistance. In the late nineteenth and early twentieth centuries, when many other advanced countries were developing interventionist social policies, public opinion in the United States continued to be hostile to replacement of residual, public assistance programmes. Relief was believed to lead to individual and social degeneration in which any benefits were far outweighed by resulting evils.[17] In the early twentieth century, the creation of a modern form of American social welfare seemed far from inevitable. It was not until the poverty caused by the depression of the thirties appeared so clearly to exceed the power of individuals to cope with it, that major collectivist action occurred. Franklin Roosevelt's Message to Congress in June 1934, with its concept of *social* security, marked a watershed in American social policy. He stated, 'Among our objectives I place the security of the men, women and children of the nation first . . . People . . . want some safeguard against misfortunes which cannot be wholly eliminated in this man-made world of ours.' Enactment of insurance-based unemployment and pension schemes followed in the Social Security Act of 1935, which was to form the basis for subsequent social legislation in the decades ahead.

Viewed from the eighties, the New Deal provided only a rudimentary system of welfare, but its provisions were seen as adequate until poverty was 'rediscovered' in the early sixties. Michael Harrington's *The Other America* (1962) aroused the public conscience with its view of a veritable modern poor farm inhabited by society's rejects and failures. Rhetoric by Presidents Kennedy and Johnson on the creation of the Great Society also helped foster an optimistic expectation that the wealth and social-science expertise of the nation, when harnessed in a War on Poverty, would end such deprivation. The disorder attendant on the Civil Rights Movement of the sixties was later seen by some as a significant cause of this expansion of welfare, in that it was a means of regulating the poor, 'a political response to political disorder'.[18] Less controversial was the perception that the movement indirectly strengthened the War on Poverty in that it helped to produce a more egalitarian climate of public opinion, heightened social expectations of the poor, and provided activists to help realize them through giving information on welfare entitlements. As a result of the War on Poverty, case loads doubled and the numbers of people under the official poverty line halved. But even this expansion still left the USA towards the bottom end of the international league table among industrial nations' social welfare spending.[19] The pattern of provision also shifted away from pre-dominantly insurance-based schemes towards assistance.

The social optimism that had underpinned the expanded welfare provision of the Kennedy and Johnson years was not sustained. Those who were relieved of poverty may have appreciated the benefits; those who financed the welfare too often saw only the effect on the taxes they were required to pay. Traditional hostility to government also played its part in undermining the vision of the sixties. In the economically uncertain years of the seventies and eighties it was replaced by a much more cautious incrementalism in social welfare. There was a widespread yet amorphous feeling that a 'welfare mess' existed that needed to be corrected. In 1969 Nixon referred to the welfare system as a 'colossal failure' and, eight years later, Carter condemned it as 'too hopeless to be cured by minor modifications'.[20] This sense of disillusionment encouraged the popular reassertion of traditionally hostile attitudes to welfare; a backlash was first apparent in provincial cutbacks and anti-welfare crusades, of which the best known was that in California. Ronald Reagan's platform, in his election as Californian Governor in 1966, contained a promise to eliminate 'welfare freeloaders'. During his governorship (which ran until 1974), his state passed the Welfare Reform Act which included provisions to cut fraud and restrict eligibility. Later, in 1978, Californian voters approved Proposition 13 which reduced property taxes by 30 per cent and led to wide-spread cutbacks in welfare. A national poll at that time showed that 57 per cent of the American people would have been in favour of it in their own state. Even before these very visible welfare cuts, reci-pients of public assistance programmes were being squeezed. Means tests became more stringent as states refused to adjust the qualifying level to allow for the increase in the cost of living that had resulted from inflation. By 1981 the average entry point to the central policy for combating family poverty – Aid to Families with Dependent Children (AFDC) – had fallen to only 57 per cent of the official poverty level. And in the worst state this was only 26 per cent. Such discrepancies have persisted: in January 1987 a family of four in California or New York might receive in AFDC payments as much as 26 per cent of the average state income, or as little as 7 per cent in Alabama or Mississippi.[21]

Workfare rather than welfare was another consequence of the changed climate of opinion. As early as 1969 President Nixon had stated that 'what America needs now is not more welfare but more workfare'.[22] Work programmes had been started in the Community Work and Training Program of 1962. This *permitted* states to establish work and training programmes for AFDC recipients; it allowed them to work off their benefits in workfare. Five years later the Work Incentive Program (WIN) modified and expanded the earlier programme through *obligating* states to provide employment programmes for AFDC recipients, although exemptions on the categories of recipients brought into the scheme blunted the scheme's impact. Further amendments in the late sixties and seventies to the WIN programmes oscillated between an emphasis on providing training and support services, and on immediate job placement. The decisive legislative reform came in the Omnibus and Budget Reconciliation Act of 1981, which introduced fundamental changes to AFDC and WIN. All able-bodied AFDC applicants, except mothers with children under six years old, were required to register for job training or employment. States could choose from several options in their programmes for these welfare recipients including WIN, Community Work Experience Programs, and Job Search. In addition, states were given the option of using AFDC benefits as a wage subsidy to encourage private employers to hire such welfare recipients. By 1985, thirty-six states were operating a job search programme, under which both AFDC applicants and recipients participated for several weeks. The best results appear to have been when this was operated as a predominantly *voluntary* or *'new-style'* form of workfare, when the programme tended to cream off the most job-ready. Under the Community Work Experience Program a *compulsory*, *'old-style'* workfare was usual under which welfare recipients worked off their benefits in unpaid jobs, usually in the community. West Virginia was the best-known example of a state running this as a mandatory state-wide programme. Programmes that combined different elements of the provisions of the 1981 act were termed WIN Demonstration Projects, and by 1984 twenty states were involved in these.[23] One such programme, combining an obligatory two-week job search with a follow up period of compulsory, unpaid work experience, was the Arkansas WORK scheme. This was set up in 1982 and operated in some, but not all, of its constituent counties. Similarly, San Diego in southern California has administered a mandatory job search programme run in practical workshop style, followed by a compulsory, experimental work-experience programme of thirteen weeks for those unplaced in a job.[24]

Given the anti-welfare ethos in the USA, workfare has attracted increased support; it has been seen as a way out of long-term welfare dependency providing a half-way house to economic independence. There have been growing anxieties in Reaganite America over the alleged existence of an 'underclass' of Blacks and Hispanics who were permanent recipients of welfare.[25] These fears have fuelled recent moves to stiffen and extend workfare provisions. AFDC recipients were seen as a prime target for workfare for a number of reasons, not all of them mutually consistent with each other. First, the cost of such support had risen alarmingly, from $4.9 billion in 1970 to $14.5 billion in 1984. Second, about half the states had now extended AFDC to two-parent families if the main breadwinner was without work. Although this provision concerned less than one-tenth of such families, the extension of welfare to the unemployed *male* brought the question of the necessity of preserving work-incentives to the forefront of discussion on welfare. Third, there was a perception – fostered by the political right – that 'traditional' family structures were breaking down. By 1984 there were 3.2 million households headed by a single female who were receiving Aid to Families with Dependent Children.[26] Confusion over the meaning of this statistic centred over whether this was a phenomenon to be explained in social terms (a question of family structure), or alternatively whether it was really an economic issue (a question of income support). Whichever answer was preferred, each gave ample space for moral concerns to confuse the debate still further with anxieties over such issues as divorce or illegitimacy, which were then linked to the more fundamental issue of welfare dependency. Finally, an increase in the proportion of *independent* working mothers to more than half of those with children under six led to a questioning of the customary exclusion from workfare programmes of *welfare* mothers with children under six years old. As a result there has been a weakening of the restrictions of workfare in AFDC. For example, a recent workfare programme in New Jersey – REACH – requires AFDC mothers to work if their children are aged two years or over.[27]

Two recently instituted workfare programmes, which catered for AFDC mothers, clearly illustrated some of their advantages and disadvantages. California's GAIN began in 1985 as a mandatory state-wide programme. This Greater Avenues to Independence programme applied to all welfare recipients who were not sick, handicapped, or the parents of pre-school children. It provided for up to two years of state-subsidized job training, education, childcare and transportation, as well as reduced welfare payments. While the relatively generous incentives offered have meant that many on welfare have reacted positively to the scheme, GAIN has encountered real difficulties. The main problem has been that receipts from low-paid work were only marginally higher than welfare payments while expenses are significantly higher.[28] A similar programme in New York City has found it difficult to provide for more than a small minority of AFDC mothers with much other than 'busy work' which has not inculcated the skills necessary for the labour market. After sixteen months of operation, the programme had enrolled only one-fifth of those eligible and, of those, only one-tenth had made the transition to full-time work.[29]

Workfare schemes in the USA are neither universal nor uniform so that evaluation of their successes and failures is problematic. There appears to be a trend away from old-style workfare (where welfare recipients were obligated to work off their benefit) to new-style workfare (where participants are involved in a wide variety of job search, work training or experience). There is some evidence to suggest that the latter increasingly involves volunteers rather than conscripts. Some of the earlier criticisms of the older type of programmes have therefore lost their force. It was said of them that people were obligated to work, but did not get the benefits of work in that a welfare cheque was no substitute for wages. Other allegations still have some credibility whether the scheme is old or new: employment in menial jobs does not necessarily enhance self-esteem or develop the skills to assist the individual in graduating to independent employment. And new-style workfare has operated most successfully in precisely those areas where arguably it was needed least. For example, the Massachusetts Employment and Training Choices Program was set up in 1983 in order to overcome educational and skill deficiencies among welfare recipients, whilst at the same time giving sufficient support services with childcare and transportation, as well as with cash benefits, to enable volunteers to make the transition from welfare to independent employment. It has been remarkably successful in doing so, but arguably this has been less the result of the programme than of full employment in the state. The Massachusetts programme saved the state considerable sums of money through shortening the welfare roll, but in many other states, providing meaningful training employment and training schemes has proved to be both a difficult exercise, and one that has been very expensive. Where there is high unemployment, schemes may in any case attract the criticism that there is a displacement effect, so that conscripts are substituted for independent labour.

Despite these well-publicized difficulties public support for workfare has remained strong, since welfare recipients are seen as owing society work. At the political level, a consensus has begun to emerge among state governors and members of Congress on the desirability of welfare reform based on workfare. A number of competing bills proposing an extension of workfare programmes have therefore been introduced in Congress during 1987. Some provisions are advantageous to the welfare client, but the increasing force of the New Right in the USA has coloured much of the proposed legislation. The value of workfare is seen by the political right as a reassertion of the work ethic which it alleges has been eroded by generous social benefits. In this view social policy has increased dependency not decreased poverty.

Political discussion in the United States has become increasingly polarized on questions concerning the interaction of welfare with economic and social developments. The right alleges that traditional family values have disintegrated, as is shown by the growth of one-parent families; that voluntary youth unemployment has risen; and that economic dependency has increased. All this is attributed to over-generous or misconceived welfare provision. Charles Murray's *Losing Ground* was probably the most contentious example of this type of writing from the New Right. He has asserted that it is the poor themselves (and not the taxpayer) who will benefit most from welfare cutbacks. Scrapping the federal income-support system for those of working age, he has argued, would allow the 'working poor' to be 'radically changed for the better', in terms of the respect and status that they would then be accorded within their own communities.[30] In contrast, those on the left have argued that serious poverty, hardship and inequality have continued despite the combined impact of local, state and federal welfare programmes. They have also minimized the adverse effects that welfare is alleged to have had on labour supply, and pointed to the importance of non-welfare influences on changes in family structure.[31]

Predicaments and Responses

This debate between liberals and conservatives in Reaganite America has influenced Thatcherite Britain as did the American War on Poverty twenty years before. Then, there was a substantial impact in the creation in Britain of Educational Priority Areas, the Urban Programme, Housing Action Areas, and Community Action Programmes.[32] In the late eighties, American theory and practice has had a marked influence in such areas as Job Search in workfare, the relationship of city schools to local industry, or the concept of health maintenance organizations. More pervasively, in each country the New Right has changed expectations of social welfare. It has applied severe cost-containment to public services, thus lowering their quality, and thereby encouraged the further expansion of the private welfare sector.[33] The much greater role in social welfare of private agencies in the United States, where very large sums of public money are routinely channelled through non-public bodies, has influenced some 'privatization' initiatives by the Conservative government in Britain. A blurring of the public–private spheres is a consequence of this and is one which can lead to difficult issues. (Poor standards of provision in privately run old people's homes in receipt of considerable sums of public money, for instance, have raised important issues both of what is an acceptable standard of care, and of financial accountability to the public.[34]) In both the USA and Britain a certain lop-sidedness has arisen in social welfare provision.

In the USA there is an obvious duality in welfare since some benefits are insurance-based while others take the form of public assistance.[35] The former have tended to have a broad social entitlement, they have not been means-tested, and they have been insulated against cuts both by the status of recipients and by the activities of their organized pressure groups. In contrast, assistance programmes have been targeted on the poor, means-tested and repeatedly cut back. The value of their benefits has been eroded by inflation, with fiscal parsimony supported by public suspicion of fraud and/or waste. It is only assistance that is termed 'welfare' and held in low public esteem. The British welfare system is more unified, yet some of the same socio-economic forces can be seen to have been at work, in protecting services that benefit a wide constituency which includes the mass of middle-class voters. It is obvious that, for example, supplementary benefit levels have been far more vulnerable to economic constraints than pensions.[36] In 1987, the newly elected Conservative government in Britain preferred the option of tax cuts to the full protection of standards and services in welfare.

In Sweden the electorate in 1985 gave a clear vote to retain the present generous system of universal welfare provision rather than cut tax rates that are the highest in Europe. The system of income-related benefits in Sweden has resulted in a wide and effective coalition of interest groups in defence of welfare. The contrast with Britain (with respect to the recipients of selective benefits whose interests are politically vulnerable) has been quite clear, but that with the USA has been even more marked. Although there has been some interaction between the Swedish and American welfare experience – as in the Swedish education programme of 1950–64 which introduced comprehensive schools on the American model – the differences have remained more compelling than the similarities. Despite the economic similarity between the two countries, in that both are capitalist economies, there are contrasting forms of welfare: in Sweden nearly all welfare comes through public agencies whereas in the United States the system is much more fragmented and a complex of private agencies plays an important role.

An explanation for differing models of welfare in terms of a country's political structure, ideology and social conditions is helpful here.[37] Sweden is a unitary state, geographically compact and socially relatively homogeneous, with a developed tradition of collectivism in social policy. In contrast, the USA is a federal country with a much more complicated political structure, in which the American people continue to adhere to an ideology antagonistic to public interventionism. A population of varied race, when combined with the diverse conditions of a huge country, also makes the formulation of aims in social policy problematic. Building a consensus is therefore difficult and, as a result, periodic developments in American welfare policy have tended to be the result of extreme circumstances, rather than having the gradualist and incrementalist character of Swedish ones.

In this respect, the political and social conditions of Sweden and Britain have been more similar, and their welfare developments in the more distant past rather more alike. Both countries were innovators, in that Britain pioneered a national unemployment insurance scheme and Sweden a pension scheme for *all* its citizens. In each country a gradual and sequential series of developments in social policy has converted an undifferentiated welfare provision through the Poor Law into a differentiated system of income maintenance for varied problems. [38] But each has retained a residual (and stigmatized) sector: in Sweden one in twenty claimants still receives social assistance; and in Britain a much larger proportion of the population have had to have recourse to supplementary benefit. And both countries have found that their social problems and inequities have been more severe than were once optimistically envisaged, and that these have persisted – though to a diminished extent – in spite of advanced welfare provision. In the more recent past the two countries have diverged in their policies towards welfare and the labour market. Although both countries have devoted the same proportion of GDP to labour market policies (2.9 per cent in 1985), Sweden has spent seven-tenths of that on interventions to increase employment, whereas Britain has used that proportion on unemployment benefit, and only three-tenths on active intervention. And while Sweden has provided an 80 per cent replacement ratio of unemployment compensation to wages, Britain has fallen well below the OECD average of 70 per cent. [39] More recently, however, initiatives in employment policy in Britain have suggested that it has learned from Sweden, as in the creation in 1987 of an integrated Employment Service (handling benefits *and* training and employment schemes for the unemployed), and the provision of youth training together with the ending of benefits for school-leavers.

Common predicaments rather than common responses are usually more obvious in the welfare experience of the USA, Sweden and Britain. A comparison of the recent adoption of workfare in these three countries as a response to unemployment, for example, indicates the different traditions that have shaped their varied implementation. The work ethic in the USA has led to a greater readiness – on the part both of the public and of participants – to support schemes that would appear quite punitive to British eyes. This has been reinforced by the more limited benefit coverage of the unemployed in the USA. In both countries about half the unemployed receive insurance benefits, but whereas in Britain the remainder receive supplementary benefits (now income support), in the United States those without work are not eligible as a group for cash public assistance.[40] And in Sweden, a corporatist tradition has facilitated a much greater willingness to support the concept of workfare by the labour movement, and to participate in the schemes by individuals. In contrast the British trade union movement has been very suspicious of any element of compulsion in the new training and employment schemes.

A certain limited parallelism has been obvious in the long-term history of comparative social welfare, in that a period of expansion, from the end of the Second World War to the early seventies, has been followed by one of retrenchment. In 1950 4 per cent of the population in the USA and in Britain were receiving cash welfare assistance, whereas by 1971 the former had a figure of 7 per cent and the latter one of 8 per cent, while Sweden at that date had 6 per cent.[41] This expansionism was a general feature of developed economies at this time; social expenditure was the fastest growing component in public expenditure between 1960 and 1981. In nineteen OECD countries social expenditure as a percentage of gross domestic product rose from 13 to 26 per cent in this period (see Table 1, line 4). Years of growth in welfare spending were followed, however, by those of retrenchment following the oil crises of 1973–4 and 1978–9. Within this overall pattern there was diversity. By 1981 five countries – of which Sweden was one – had social

expenditures of over 30 per cent of GDP. The UK and the USA had
more modest proportions with 24 and 21 per cent respectively
(Table 1, column iii). The UK was on the lower end of this growth
in social expenditures but still found it difficult to cut back (Table 1,
columns iv and v). An important reason for this was the comparatively high rate of UK unemployment associated with a low rate of
economic growth.

Table 1: Social Expenditures of Selected Countries, 1960–81

	Social expenditure[1] as % of GDP at current prices			Annual growth rate of deflated social expenditure[2]	
	(i) 1960	(ii) 1975	(iii) 1981	(iv) 1960–75	(v) 1975–81
UK	13.9	22.4	23.7	5.9	1.8
USA	10.9	20.8	20.8	8.0	3.2
Sweden	15.4	26.8	33.4	7.9	4.7
OECD average (unweighted)	13.1	23.9	25.6	8.4	4.8

Source: *Social Expenditure 1960–81* (OECD, Paris, 1985), p. 21.
Notes:
1. Public expenditure on: education; pensions; health; unemployment compensation;
sickness; maternity or temporary disablement benefits; family and child allowances;
other income maintenance programmes or welfare services.
2. Social expenditure measured at constant GDP prices.

The direction of welfare expenditures in OECD countries has
also shown a similar overall pattern but with varied emphases in
detailed provision. In all countries, health, education and pensions
comprised about four-fifths of expenditure throughout the period.
The sixties were a decade of general expansion in education with
extended periods of schooling and expanded higher education.
Thereafter, educational spending was much more tightly controlled
than health or pensions, in part because of demographic changes
bringing about smaller enrolment in educational institutions.
Throughout the period health spending was buoyant as a result of
public health initiatives and the spread of best practices. But the area
of spending that continued to be largest was pensions. Improved

benefits, an increase in older age groups, and indexation during a period of inflation, were significant causes of this, but it is also the case that pensions involve long-term contracts and are therefore inflexible in the short term. In contrast, expenditures on unemploy-

Table 2: *Types of Expenditure as Percentage of Total Social Expenditures in Selected Countries*

		UK	USA	Sweden	OECD average (unweighted)
Education[1]					
	1960	26.6	33.0	29.9	27.3
	1975	30.3	29.2	21.0	24.9
	1981	24.5	26.4	19.8	22.7
Health[2]					
	1960	24.5	11.9	22.1	19.0
	1975	22.3	26.9	17.5	22.4
	1981	22.8	20.2	26.6	22.7
Pensions[3]					
	1960	29.5	38.5	28.6	32.0
	1975	28.2	33.1	30.5	31.2
	1981	31.2	35.6	35.3	38.8
Unemployment[4]					
	1960	1.4	5.5	1.3	2.6
	1975	3.1	5.6	0.9	3.7
	1981	5.9	2.4	1.5	4.0
Other Social Expenditure					
	1960	18.0	11.1	18.1	19.1
	1975	16.1	5.2	30.1	17.8
	1981	15.6	15.4	16.8	16.8

Source: *Social Expenditure 1960–90* (OECD, Paris, 1985), p. 21.
Notes on principal items of expenditure:
1. Pre-primary, primary, secondary, tertiary education and services.
2. Medical, dental, para-medical and public health services.
3. Old age, disability, survivors and government pensions.
4. Insurance, and other governmental schemes to compensate for loss of income during unemployment.

ment compensation were very modest in scale, although since 1981 the rise in unemployment has made this much more important. Table 2 shows the UK's experience in relation to that of other developed countries in these areas of social expenditure.

This very brief comparative review has suggested that there have been three main stages in the evolution of the modern welfare state: experimentation has given way to consolidation and extension, and then to a period of reconsideration. In this latest stage the feeling of *economic* crisis in welfare is now considered to have 'peaked'.[42] In the late eighties concern is focused principally on the need for *structural* adjustments to increase flexibility and efficiency in social welfare so that, in a colder economic climate, old programmes can continue and new needs be met. Longer-term planning than that which operated in the hectic expansion of the sixties and seventies is seen as essential in the allocation of scarce resources. OECD countries face three principal challenges in the late eighties and beyond. These arise from the increasing number of the *long-term* unemployed; the rise in the ratio of pensioners to people of working age, and the huge extra burden of health care necessitated by older people. In this respect, British attempts to contain costs in the National Health Service, or to reform pensions and social security arrangements, fit into an international context of similar concerns. These attempts to restructure British welfare in the eighties have certain parallels with a much earlier period of Victorian reform to which we now turn.

III

Victorian and Edwardian Welfare Policies

During the century and a half from the 1830s to the 1980s there were three periods when state intervention in British social policy significantly increased. The first of these occurred in the 1830s and 1840s, and the second in the Edwardian years at the beginning of the twentieth century. Fundamental in the first burst of reforming activity was the New Poor Law of 1834 which centred round the workhouse system. It gave conditional welfare for a minority, with public assistance as the price of social stigma and loss of voting rights. Some Edwardian reforms still retained conditions on take-up, as in the first state old-age pensions in 1908, where tests of means and character eligibility were reminiscent of the Poor Law. Three years later there was a radical departure in the national scheme for insurance against ill-health and unemployment, which conferred benefits as a result of contributions. This was still a selective scheme in that it was limited to a section of the male population and entirely left out dependent women and children. It was not until the last of our three periods of expansion – that of the 1940s – that universality in provision was seen as a crucial ingredient in social welfare. Many of these later welfare provisions were either a reaction to, or a continuation of, policies that had begun in the Victorian and Edwardian periods. And the discussions that shaped their creation often showed similar grounds for contention to those surfacing in arguments over social welfare today.

The Victorian Poor Law and Workhouse

Enacted three years before Victoria came to the throne in 1837, the New Poor Law of 1834 is a particularly apposite place to begin a

[29]

survey of welfare. The fundamental objective of the 1834 Act – in attempting to inaugurate more economical relief in England and Wales[1] to replace what was perceived as a wasteful and over-generous system – has a broad similarity to reforming efforts in the 1980s to produce a leaner welfare state. There are parallels between its values and those of the libertarian right in the 1980s. The circumstances of its creation and implementation exposed with unusual clarity some important issues that were to recur in the evolution of the British welfare state. Amongst these were the stigmatizing character of highly selective welfare; the large discretionary powers possessed by bureaucrats and the problems of accountability that these raised; and conflicts over policy and finance arising from the duality of local and central administration. It is also important to appreciate that the 1834 Poor Law endured in statutory form until 1948, so that later welfare legislation was often introduced to modify, extend or abolish aspects of this fundamental piece of social legislation. Further, many popular attitudes to twentieth-century welfare are impossible to understand without reference to folk memories of the workhouses established after 1834, and the associated system of deterrent, conditional poor relief. Indeed, a study of the Poor Law's historical influence on social policy may suggest a model of welfare development as one of retrospection in which reaction against the perceived past was central to the creation of future policy.[2]

In the two decades before 1834 agitation against the existing system of public welfare, under the parochially based Old Poor Law, took the form of criticism about allegedly over-generous welfare payments and the unbearably heavy costs this imposed on local ratepayers, on whom the finance of poor relief fell. In reality, neither the relief nor the rates were unprecedentedly large but economic depression made the burden *appear* intolerable. Worse, it was argued that the economy itself was being harmed by the system of relief: work-incentives were being eroded by the small – or non-existent – margin between the labourers' wages and relief payments adjusted to family size.[3] The portrayal of a pauperized labourer, encouraged by welfare to prefer dependent breeding to independent labour, entered the stage-cast of welfare mythology through the purple prose of the Royal Commission on the Poor Laws of 1832–4.

This inquiry, the first in British history to conduct an extensive social investigation into the available evidence, has quite rightly been called both wildly unhistorical and wildly unstatistical,[4] since the Commission either ignored or manipulated its data to reach pre-determined conclusions. Its objectives were to cut the costs of welfare through conditional, deterrent relief and thus to relieve the taxpayers' burdens, restore work-incentives, and re-impose a proper subordination upon the labouring classes.

The conclusions of the Commission were swiftly translated into one of the most important pieces of social legislation in the nineteenth century – the Poor Law Amendment Act of 1834. It has been suggested that there was an obvious link between this social reform and contemporary economic conditions. This kind of socio-economic relationship was also to be apparent in later 'crisis' periods in the history of welfare. In this context it is interesting to reflect on a certain parallelism discernible between the 'tax backlashes' of the 1830s and 1970s and subsequent attempts at redrawing the frontiers of welfare. Or, to take another example, to see in debates over revised benefits during the depressed years of the inter-war period a recurrence of the intense concern over the maintenance of work-incentives for the insured population that had been prominent in the 1830s discussion over reformed relief payments. In each of these later periods the concept of the 'less eligibility' of the welfare recipient in comparison with the independent population was prominent. This idea – of the welfare recipient being given a lower standard of living than the independent worker – was first fully worked out in terms of social policy, in the New Poor Law of 1834.

Less eligibility in this 1834 reform was conceived in psychological rather than material terms, since the conditions of life of the independent labouring poor were so low that further deprivation under a publicly administered scheme could only have produced scandalous conditions. The lynch-pin of reform was to be institutional relief in a workhouse run on such deterrent lines that only the truly destitute, rather than the merely poor, would accept relief on such terms. Although much contemporary criticism focused on the supposedly terrible material conditions in the workhouse, with allegations of starvation resulting from the regulation diets, this target was misplaced. The real deprivation was less in body than in mind: it derived principally from the isolation of the pauper from the community; in the classification (separation) of members of a family in different parts of the institution; the dehumanizing of inmates through the wearing of a pauper uniform; the tyranny of the clock in the regulation of the day; the purposelessness of what little activity was provided, and the monotony and boredom that yawned widely for the remainder of the day. This psychological deprivation was enhanced since an unintended consequence of the 1834 Act was that such inmates were infrequently the 'able-bodied' poor for whom the workhouse had been intended, but predominately the 'helpless' poor – the aged, the children and the sick. In concentrating on the economic implications of welfare, and thus on the able-bodied adult male, the Royal Commission had virtually ignored the principal classes of welfare recipients.[5] This emphasis on the *adult male* was to be replicated in later reforms in social policy, notably schemes of social insurance at the heart of the twentieth-century welfare state.

The concept of less eligibility, to be achieved through institutional means, owed much to Bentham's panopticon poorhouse, in which 'charity is the end; economy is but the means'.[6] But, owing mainly to the failure of the 1834 Act to modify the precarious and inequitable local system of poor rates which financed the system of poor relief, economy was the dominant influence on both means and ends. Until the 1860s the rating units were 15,000 parishes; thereafter this was changed to 600 poor-law unions. Local financial accountability was seen as imperative, and a broader and more secure economic base as undesirable, since this would be achieved through a redistribution of resources; richer areas (with fewer paupers) would then effectively subsidize impoverished ones (with many paupers). As a result of this failure to reform the basis of poor-law finances, poor rates were largely regressive and there was a tendency for the less poor to be rated to aid the really poor. The 'territorial injustices' of unequal welfare provision, discovered by social scientists as features of the mid-twentieth-century welfare state, were in fact far more obvious in Victorian Britain. Then, financial grants to improve facilities in deprived areas by central or local government (in this case the poor-law guardians), were far more limited. And the inegalitarian rating system went hand in hand with laws of settlement and removal that restricted the right to relief to the place of settlement (often that of birth, but later increasingly that of continued residence). These laws, abolished only in 1948, helped preserve geographical inequalities in the treatment received by the poor. Provision for the Victorian pauper was therefore variable; not only were resources unequal but local administrators interpreted central policies in diverse ways.

The Poor Law Amendment Act has been interpreted by some historians as a profoundly centralizing measure since it created a central poor-law board with powers to issue regulations, a team of inspectors to see that these were followed by local administrators, and district auditors to impose financial penalties if relief expenditure was not incurred justifiably. And much greater systematization in the forms of relief administration was visible at the local level in a bureaucratic uniformity of elected boards of guardians and appointed paid officials, and also in proliferating accounts and relief statements. Interpretations of the success of the reformed policies themselves differ. The main thrust of the 1834 Act had been the workhouse test, whereby indoor relief (i.e. in the workhouse) for the able-bodied poor would be so distasteful that independent labour would be preferred to welfare dependence. It follows that the undisputedly low numbers of the able-bodied in these Victorian 'bastilles' might either show the success of the policy or the preference of the guardians for an alternative – that of granting cheaper outdoor relief.[7] That such outdoor relief continued to be granted to substantial numbers of the able-bodied, thus perpetuating the system of allowances that the 1834 Act had been designed to end, suggests the continued existence of discretionary power at local level in determining relief policies. Local muscle was in part the result of the failure of the 1834 Act to give the central board powers to *compel* guardians to build a workhouse. It arose in part through the intrinsic inability of the board to frame regulations that could, on the one hand, be sufficiently flexible in their detail to take account of varied human needs and, on the other hand, be adequately legalistic in their restrictions to prevent loopholes that would undercut the main policy. And that bureaucratic ingenuity was not adequate to this task should not surprise us given the later, comparable history of supplementary benefits regulations in the 1970s.

Other parallels between the 1830s–40s and the 1970–80s are evident in similar debates over hereditary pauperism and transmitted deprivation. An anxiety among leading poor-law reformers that dependence continued in families from one generation to the next led to a view of the New Poor Law which included relief as rehabilitation. This was particularly evident in the moral and industrial training given to the young in workhouse schools. Prescriptive elements of social control were also used in the moral discrimination practised in poor-law administration: relief might be refused to the drunkard or poacher; indoor relief in the deterrent workhouse was offered to those deemed 'undeserving' – such as the unmarried mother; and outdoor relief given in their own homes to an applicant seen as one of the 'deserving' poor. The price paid for such dependency was often stigmatization, though it is clear that popular attitudes made a distinction between indoor and outdoor relief. By the end of the nineteenth century there was little or no stigma attached, for example, to an old person receiving an outdoor allowance since this was viewed as being pretty well inevitable after a lifetime of low-paid toil.

This differentiation may suggest that stigma was targeted on certain types of people, who were also prone to dependency, rather than on their connection with the Poor Law *per se*.[8] Those groups whose destitution was seen as the result of individual moral failing – feckless adults such as mothers of illegitimate children or vagrants – were given indoor relief in the workhouse. Other groups – widows, the temporarily disabled, the old – were seen as retaining respectability since their poverty was not perceived as avoidable. These groups were *not* usually relieved in the workhouse. It is, of course, problematic to what extent this connection with the workhouse was cause or effect of the stigmatizing process; over time this was likely to have become a self-reinforcing process. However, the determination of local poor-law guardians to stretch their discretionary powers to the legal limit – and frequently rather beyond this – in order to maximize discrimination in the allocation of indoor or outdoor relief to different groups, suggests that the workhouse was seen to confirm rather than cause social stigma. This interpretation receives additional support from the fate of those groups, such as children or the sick, who were forced into the institution through lack of alternative provision in the early years of the New Poor Law. Their position was increasingly recognized to be anomalous in that their social treatment did not reflect their moral status. Developments in their later treatment under the Poor Law may therefore be read in part as attempts to lessen their connection with the stigmatizing workhouse; children were sent out to elementary schools, boarded out, or relieved in separate homes, while many of the sick were later to be housed in infirmaries distinct from the main workhouse buildings. And, when the extension of the suffrage in 1867 and 1884 meant that pauper status caused the loss of the vote in practice (rather than merely in theory as in earlier years), legislation in 1885 ensured that the sick in receipt of poor relief were not disfranchised.

The New Poor Law was a last resort for the poor, and comparative studies indicate that such 'residual' forms of relief are especially prone to stigmatization. The declining proportion of the population who were paupers – down from one in twelve in 1834 to one in forty by 1901 (the end of Victoria's reign) – may have intensified this division of the population into 'us and them', and increased the burden of stigma that poor relief conferred. It is worth extending our analysis of stigma and the Poor Law briefly into the modern period since it shows the way that attitudes to one form of welfare may be transmitted to a later form of assistance, and changes in nomenclature or formal categories of relief disregarded. In the twentieth century the social taint of poor relief outlived the reign of the guardians (which came to an end in 1930), and continued into that of their successors – the Public Assistance Committees – who administered relief in the form of Transitional Payments to the unemployed whose insurance had run out. The intense resentment that this provoked indicated the continued strength of the traditional social attitude that welfare must not reduce the respectable working population to the level of the feckless. The resilience of older beliefs is shown also by adverse reactions towards modern welfare institutions housed in the bricks and mortar of the New Poor Law; for residents in old people's homes converted from such buildings, the shadow of the workhouse is still a reality.

Adverse reactions from the British labour movement to any compulsory element in modern schemes of workfare may also originate in part from the unpopular labour tests under the Poor Law, when work was exacted from able-bodied males as a test of destitution. Poor relief was given only after task work had been completed in the labour or stone yard of the workhouse. The labour test was an acknowledgement that the workhouse test was inapplicable to the conditions of industrial recession, since the number of unemployed male applicants for relief would have exceeded the capacity of the workhouse to give indoor relief. By 1852 the prohibition of outdoor relief to able-bodied men in urban and industrial areas had effectively been abandoned, but tests on such relief were imposed in the form of tasks of work such as corn grinding, wood chopping, stone breaking, or oakum picking. In practice, labour yards were characterized by great variety in the tasks imposed, the efficiency of the supervision, the hours of work, or the number of days in the week that the applicant had to attend before being granted relief. As a result of the difficulty of running a sufficiently deterrent labour yard in conjunction with the normal mixed, general workhouse, a small number of unions chose for short periods of time, between the 1870s and the 1920s, to set up an alternative in the form of specialist, able-bodied test workhouses. They imposed on the able-bodied man a sterner regime and a more severe task of work. These establishments were condemned by the Royal Commission on the Poor Laws in 1909 as not 'within the legitimate functions of a Public Assistance Authority'.[9]

Victorian Social Interventions

The New Poor Law was only the most central bureaucratic initiative of many Victorian social reforms. The extent of social intervention by the state during the 1830s and 1840s has caused one historian to interpret it as a 'revolution in government', and another to see it as forming the 'Victorian origins' of the British welfare state.[10] While the first over-dramatizes the magnitude of discontinuity with the past, and the second that of continuity with the future, each provides us with an insight into a fundamental shift in governmental responsibilities and administrative competence. Government agencies were created to regulate the Poor Law, factories, prisons, schools and asylums, and inspectors were appointed to see that centrally determined legislation and regulation were implemented at the local level. The state had increased its commitment both to regulate the deviant and to protect those (notably women and children) who were seen as too weak to defend their own interests against the pressures of the free market. Administrative historians have provided satisfactory explanations for the momentum that such reforms soon attained. An internal bureaucratic dynamic resulted from inspectors' discovery of regulatory shortcomings and of previously unknown abuses which caused further incremental change. Agreed explanations of the genesis of the *original* reforms have proved to be more difficult.

The imperatives of industrialization and of urbanization have been incorporated in both the humanitarian and the social control types of explanation. In the former kind of analysis, the existence of 'intolerable' abuses caused by the Industrial Revolution, together with an increasing concentration of the population in growing towns, self-evidently necessitated benevolent, remedial state intervention since these were beyond the powers of individuals or local bodies to redress. In the latter interpretation the traditional paternalism of a rural, agrarian Britain had been made redundant by the new class-based society. There was a countervailing need for new forms of authority to contain and control a large body of social outcasts whose life-style appeared to challenge the order, morality and work ethic of society.

In mid-Victorian England such anxiety centred on the threat that crime posed to society so that debate centred on criminal or semi-criminal groups; these were the 'dangerous classes' of criminals, together with their source of recruitment in the 'perishing classes' of destitute juveniles.[11] By the late Victorian period concern had shifted from crime to the labour market, and focused on the problem of casual labour. Charles Booth in his survey of London labour had Class A at the bottom of his social hierarchy: this included criminals, semi-criminals, loafers, and the lowest class of occasional labourers who relied on varied strategems to eke out a living, and were consequently often dependent on poor relief or charity. Unlike social commentators thirty years before, however, Booth saw Class A as 'a disgrace but not a danger'. Significantly, he also viewed it as very largely 'hereditary in character',[12] a perception that was to be held even more strongly by later commentators. By the early twentieth century the unproductive groups on the fringe of the casual labour market were termed the 'residuum' or the 'workshy'; they were seen as a parasitic group, of diminishing size, whose fecklessness was diagnosed largely in terms of character defects.[13] Historically, the groups we have briefly described were the progenitors of the modern 'underclass', discussed in recent years in Britain and the USA with equal lack of precision, and with a similar conflation of the moral with the social. Perceptions of the character of the underclass have continued to change in line with fashionable social theories: since the sixties, analyses have viewed them not through the spectacles of eugenics (as had been usual during the inter-war period), but through the culture of poverty, and hence have seen this group as a victim of demographic and/or technological change.[14] Throughout these 150 years, the alleged dependence of the underclass on welfare has been as prominent in public debate as social policy's supposed potential to reform or control.

The enactment of the New Poor Law as a response to the Swing riots of 1830 had made it clear that *one* of its intended functions was to act as a form of social control for the poor. A deterrent system of 'relief as last resort' would thus help to restore work-incentives and social order. While most historians would accept that such control was an important element in the reform, attempts to widen the hypothesis, from the control of obvious deviants such as paupers or prisoners to others such as lunatics, seem less plausible. However, with most Victorian reforms (as with modern developments such as certain supplementary benefit regulations[15]), it seems more realistic to see social control as an occasional byproduct rather than a prime intention of reform. Such discussion usefully alerts us to the need to look beyond stated objectives of reform to its concealed aims since, in most historical periods, humanitarian altruism may be seen as a scarce good. In this context, research on recent phases of the welfare state has been useful in emphasizing the complexity of legislative development, and in showing that a final consensus on reform might be the result of conflicting interests or varied intent.[16] That this was also true of Victorian reform has been exposed in investigations by historians of different ideological persuasions. For example, legislative limitation in 1844 of the hours that women should work in textile factories appears, according to newer feminist analysis, to owe much both to the conflation of moral and social concerns and to the interests of organized male labour, who thereby hoped to reduce their own hours of work. Earlier, in a traditional 'Whiggish' interpretation, it was seen as arising from a humanitarian desire to protect the weak.

The influence of ideology on social policy also remains contentious. Nowhere is this more evident than in the long-running debate on Victorian collectivism. How and why such momentous state intervention occurred in an era of supposedly *laissez-faire* philosophy has received varied answers. (Comparable problems of explanation are produced by the paradox of increasing state intervention in the 1980s, when prevailing political rhetoric also extols the free market.) Dicey's famous labelling of the period from 1825 to 1870 as an age of Benthamite individualism has led to some neat footwork by later historians attempting to reconcile this with much collectivist activity. On the one hand, Benthamism has been incorporated into both camps and aptly interpreted as having elements of individualism *and* collectivism. On the other hand, such intellectual influences have all but disappeared from view in the type of administrative argument previously discussed, through emphasis on 'pressure of facts' as the cause of social action. An extension of this type of analysis has been to discern a hierarchy of bureaucratic interventionism of increasing intensity, and thus a continuum of individualism with later collectivism. Another solution has been to separate social from economic issues, on a rather arbitrary basis, and to view interventionism as directed at the former and *laissez-faire* as concerned with the latter. An ingenious – but only partial – alternative explanation has emphasized the role of state interventionism in removing obstacles from the free market.[17] After several decades of debate, none of these varied hypotheses commands the field, but there is some residual agreement by historians on the predominantly reluctant nature of Victorian collectivism, on the *ad hoc* incremental nature of many of its reforms, and on the conservative or limited nature of others.

These last three characteristics of Victorian interventionism are illustrated particularly clearly in the field of public health. To a twentieth-century observer the reasons for preventive state intervention might well seem overwhelming but at the time this was only grudgingly conceded over several decades. Great Britain's population had doubled in the first half of the nineteenth century and the rate of growth of many urban areas was even higher; the inhabitants of Leeds and Birmingham increased threefold; Glasgow, Manchester and Liverpool fourfold; and Bradford eightfold. The impact of this demographic revolution on very limited water supplies, drains and sewers was to produce an overcrowded, insanitary urban environment with appallingly high mortality rates. In the 1830s Edwin Chadwick, of the Poor Law Commission, was alerted to the magnitude of the problem by the *economic* cost to public funds of disease; illness was a significant cause of pauperism, and thus of dependence on the poor rates. His ensuing research into the problem resulted in the highly influential *Report on the Sanitary Condition of the Labouring Population of Great Britain* (1842), which firmly established a statistical connection between environment and disease. Sales were unprecedentedly high – an estimated 100,000 copies, which compared well with the equivalent twentieth-century 'official bestseller', the Beveridge Report of 1942. Action on the radical conclusions of Chadwick's report was to take a quarter of a century and effective action another decade after that. Leaving aside medical difficulties (over the exact causes of the diseases that ravaged the Victorian towns), and also the technical engineering problems (of manufacturing an efficient sanitary network), we concentrate here on financial, political and ideological factors that inhibited state action on this – as on so many other – subjects.

The prevailing contemporary assumption was that any public action to improve this situation would be taken locally not centrally. But the impediments to such initiatives were formidable. A precarious and inequitable rating base made a call for inactivity seductive in local politics. 'The people were more solicitous about draining rates from their pockets than draining the streets,' commented a Leeds councillor in 1844.[18] At the local level the chaos of overlapping administrative bodies, with jealously guarded interests of patronage and power, prevented rapid or decisive action even on the few occasions when this was recognized by the community as imperative. Outbreaks of cholera, notably those in 1831–2 and 1848–9, created sufficient terror in the propertied classes for *national* initiatives in public health to be taken, although they were to be implemented by local boards of health. Significantly, these enactments of 1831 and 1848 were largely permissive. Indeed, Disraeli's view that 'permissive legislation is the characteristic of a free people'[19] was almost universally held at this time. The ideology of *laissez-faire* extended even to sewage; *The Times* suggested in 1854 that every man had the right to sit on his own dung heap! It took years of patiently accumulated evidence by John Simon (as Medical Officer first to the central Board of Health and then to the Medical Department of the Privy Council) for a change in attitude to be affected. In 1865 Simon argued that 'it ought no longer to be discretional in a place whether that place shall be kept filthy or not . . . The language of the law besides making it a power should also name it a *duty* to proceed for the removal of nuisances.'[20] In the following year the Sanitary Act laid down such a duty and *inter alia* extended the power of central over local government in enforcing this, while the Public Health Act of 1875 systematically enumerated a wide range of public health duties for local bodies.

By the 1870s there was a greater readiness to recognize the role of state action, not only in the negative sense of removing nuisances, but also with more positive interventions. Older ideas on *laissez-faire* had certainly not disappeared but the presumption that central governmental inactivity was necessarily always the best course was no longer an unthinking axiom in public affairs. The tide was beginning to turn, although adherence to collectivist values was more limited than a retrospective view might suggest. Belief in the desirability of voluntaryism remained strong. Even when voluntary action had proved inadequate so that collectivist action was deemed necessary – as in the field of education, with the Elementary Education Act of 1870 – public intervention was to supplement and not to replace private activity. This view of the limited role of the state remained influential in the Edwardian period in spite of increasing public commitment to social welfare.

The Edwardian Social Service State

Seen in international perspective, the Edwardian 'social service' state provided the first experimental phase of the British welfare state. These reforms of the Liberal ministry of 1906–14 significantly increased central intervention in social reform. In evolutionary accounts of the rise of the welfare state it has proved only too easy to emphasize the inevitability of these social policies on a broad road of increasing collectivism, since the objective of the social service state was to deliver minimal standards to selected groups, while that of the later welfare state was to provide optimal ones, comprehensively. Yet, when placed in the detailed political, economic and social context of Edwardian Britain, explanations of the origins and character of such reforms become more complex. It then appears not only that few contemporaries viewed them as an interim launching pad for even more state intervention in the future, but also that these social policies owed much to the past.

The extent to which Edwardian policies were shaped by past concerns, constraints and attitudes is perhaps less easy to appreciate at first sight than the break they made with what had gone before. Two enactments – that of 1911, providing contributory insurance for health and unemployment, and that of 1908, giving non-contributory pensions on a basis that did not compromise civic rights as had earlier poor relief – appear most obviously as principled precedents for modern welfare provision. However, it is important to notice that the basis of health insurance rested on the same kind of dualism that we have noted in the earlier 1870 Education Act; state action in 1911 'filled in the gaps' of the voluntary provision made by the approved societies, and also relied on them for its administration. Coexisting with a continuation of the Victorian practice of central enactment but local implementation went an increased centralism in such measures as old-age pensions or unemployment insurance. And, paradoxically, a continued Conservative reluctance to reform the basis of local finance through rate equalization, and thus provide sufficient resources for increased social policies, forced a more radical, central alternative of a 'progressive' income tax in 1909. This is a nice example of the way in which the past may mould both positively and negatively. Much social welfare provision may be seen as a product of this kind of dialectic with the past; the relationship of the 'Victorian' Poor Law to Edwardian provision illustrates the kind of continuities and discontinuities involved.

Edwardian services were often old rather than new in their functions, replicating those already available under the Poor Law, as in assistance to the sick, to children and to the old. The creation of alternatives to the guardians has been seen as the 'inevitable' result of an extended suffrage.[21] Contemporary support can be adduced for a *long-term* interpretation linking the advent of democracy with the creation of non-stigmatized welfare, as in the well-known speech of the radical Joseph Chamberlain in 1885. He argued that domestic legislation would in future be 'more directed to what he called social questions than has hitherto been the case' and asked, 'What ransom will property pay for the security which it enjoys?' suggesting, in answer to his own question, that 'we shall hear a great deal more about the obligations of property, and we shall not hear so much about its rights'. Yet a *short-term* version of this interpretation has difficulty in explaining the time lag between the extension of the suffrage (in 1867 and 1884) and a belated legislative response. Also, it encounters problems in accounting for the small role given at this time to social questions in party electoral manifestos, or in evaluating the mixed attitudes that new working-class voters displayed towards state welfare. Suspicion and hostility were shown by members of the working class to more intrusive state measures such as compulsory elementary education, but coexisting with this was gratitude for ameliorative measures – such as school meals or pensions – that lessened the difficulties of hard lives.[22] Interestingly, the complicated nature of popular attitudes to welfare today is one that has attracted much recent analysis by social scientists – in this case related not to the advance of state commitments in the field of welfare, but to their retreat.

In the late Victorian era attitudes to poverty changed and this stimulated a different view of society's responsibilities to the poor. These newer ideas dated from the 1860s and 1870s,[23] but were reinforced very powerfully by the findings of the famous poverty surveys of Booth in the 1880s in London, and of Rowntree in York at the very end of the century. Poverty was redefined and rediscovered, as indeed was the case in the 1960s and, in each period, this went hand in hand with a re-evaluation of the adequacy – or rather inadequacy – of public provision for poorer groups in society. But whereas the later redefinition was relativistic in its view of poverty, that of the Victorian age attempted some absolute measure by means of a poverty line. This had the merit of targeting attention on the unexpected amount of deprivation: the shocking relevation that nearly *one-third* of the population were below the poverty line, as against only *one-fortieth* who were receiving poor relief, forced a re-examination of existing methods of treating the poor. Social scientists had succeeded in 'remoralizing' the poor, since there was found to be in existence a large class who were poor but not pauperized.[24] And, in showing that common causes of poverty lay in general economic factors (e.g. unemployment or low wages), as well as in the individual moral failings emphasized in the New Poor Law, the class of deserving poor – to whom help should be given – was correspondingly expanded. These were the potential beneficiaries of the new state provision of the Edwardian period.

This expansion of collectivist action was also a response to international economic and political pressures. Beginning in 1870, with debates over the need for an improved system of education to produce more efficient workers, there was awareness that Great Britain's industrial supremacy was being challenged by competitors, and that social reform was needed to buttress it. The realization that state action was needed to improve not only the mental, but also the physical, capabilities of the working class was stimulated by the poor physical condition of army recruits for the Boer War. Legislation on the provision of free school meals in 1906, and of school medical inspection in the following year, was a direct result of findings by the 1904 Interdepartmental Committee on Physical Deterioration that had followed the disasters of the Boer War of 1899–1902. That imperial interests in Africa and elsewhere were linked to social welfare was widely accepted, although there was disagreement among such 'social imperialists' as to the relationships involved. Working-class welfare was dependent on imperial strength, according to Conservatives in the Tariff Reform League who argued that tariffs on non-empire goods would finance reforms such as old-age pensions. On the other hand, Liberals and socialists tended to argue that the future of the empire depended on a healthy race, and hence necessitated improved conditions for the working class. But that empire and social reform *always* went hand in hand has been challenged recently by the view that the 1906 Liberal ministry's tolerance of capital exports inhibited spending on social welfare and, especially, on schools.[25]

Internationally, the welfare of workers was the focus of much greater attention in the late nineteenth and early twentieth centuries. Investment in human capital to enhance efficiency was seen by both governments and employers as vital to survival in a more competitive world economy. A further motive was discernible in German and British social insurance in a desire to counter 'the socialist threat', and to win support from the working class, but without increasing fiscal demands on the state.[26] This counterpoint between socialist and capitalist pressures for reform was central to the complex orchestration that produced the Edwardian social service state. It was a good example of a recurrent theme in the history of welfare in that radical action stemmed from a conservative rationale. The desirability of a pre-emptive first strike against socialism appeared clear as, for example, in the arguments in 1895 of A. J. Balfour, who became Prime Minister in 1902: 'Social legislation, as I conceive it, is not merely to be distinguished from socialist legislation, but is its direct opposite and its most effective antidote.'[27] The election of thirty Labour MPs in 1906 put pressure on the Liberal ministry to intervene more actively in social issues, and thus enhanced the influence of the New Liberalism within the Liberal party. Later, Lloyd George's proposals for workers' insurance can be seen as motivated in part by a desire to 'dish the Webbs', and pre-empt certain of the socialistic conclusions of the Minority Report on the Poor Law of 1909. In part it also arose belatedly from the competitive urge to outdo, rather than merely imitate, earlier reforms in Germany – Britain's economic and imperial rival.[28] Thus, there should not only be health insurance but the novel provision of unemployment insurance as well.

This radical strand in Liberal social policy was evident in decisive action in the labour market, where the adult male worker was now affected, rather than the women and children earlier involved in keynote Victorian legislation. Limitation of miners' hours occurred in 1908; the creation of employment exchanges in 1909; and the enactment of national unemployment insurance two years later. Radical elements coexisted with conservative ones in the formulation of labour policy. A traditional economic concern to preserve work-incentives, and a moral anxiety to deter the fraudulent, were evident in the linkage of labour exchanges and unemployment insurance. The former would test willingness to work, and the latter would place a check on malingering, bogus claims and voluntary unemployment, through imposing elaborate sets of conditions on benefits.[29] The role of employers in stimulating these last two developments is significant;[30] such 'welfare capitalism' served to enhance labour's mobility and efficiency and thus to strengthen the existing social structure. Predictably, sections of the trade union movement were hostile because employment exchanges were seen as a usurpation of unions' role in the labour market. Also criticized was the imposition rather than negotiation of unemployment insurance; the regressive nature of contributions; and the inequities in benefit between different groups of workers likely to arise from the varied nature of unemployment, of which the legislation failed to take account.

The more collectivist policies envisaged or enacted at the turn of the century posed dilemmas of more than passing period interest. Could extended governmental welfare coexist with the values of a free people, or was Bismarckian social welfare only suited to a people used to 'police supervision from the cradle to the grave'?[31] Could the state intervene to help the most deprived without undercutting self-help; in particular, would non-contributory pensions parch the springs of thrift, and harm work-incentives by undercutting the less-eligibility principle of the Poor Law? Could radical social legislation be a defence against socialism without becoming socialistic? The Treasury feared in 1899 that the proposal for old-age pensions rested on a 'socialistic principle',[32] and that this was likely to prove contagious. The provisions of the Edwardian social-service state thus challenged old assumptions but gave no very clear answers about what was to replace them. Indeed, at the time, few saw the long-term implications of the precedents being established; Winston Churchill and David Lloyd George were two who did. At the Board of Trade, the former welcomed the fact that the introduction of unemployment insurance would make the old moral basis of conditional welfare redundant – 'I do not like mixing up moralities and mathematics.'[33] And in his People's Budget of 1909, Lloyd George used the budget as a subordinate instrument of welfare, introducing a progressive income tax to pay for reform. He argued that, 'This is a War Budget. It is for raising money to raise implacable warfare against poverty and squalidness.'[34] For Lloyd George, insurance was a temporary expedient[35] rather than the principled and long-term component of a welfare state. That such social reform would be a prolonged process was understood; Lloyd George discussed this explicitly when he spoke about the introduction of health insurance: 'I never said this bill was a final solution. I am not putting it forward as a complete remedy. It is one of a series. We are advancing on the road.'[36]

IV

The Emergence of the Classic Welfare State

The comparision between inter-war and post-war welfare provision has usually been too starkly drawn. The twenties and thirties have been seen as a welfare wasteland; years dominated by a series of humiliating and economical expedients to relieve the unemployed. In contrast the extensive measures of the forties have often been viewed as a Mecca of optimal welfare. Yet it is important to appreciate that there were significant advances in inter-war social policy; its scope and social expenditure increased substantially. And, while selectivity gave way to universality in post-war measures, their radical nature has been overemphasized. As in earlier years there were concerns about work-incentives, less eligibility or minimizing public expenditures. In providing a blueprint of what is termed here the 'classic welfare state', the author of the Beveridge Report of 1942 had seen its policies as developing naturally from the past. We should be aware, however, that the legislation which followed the report was not the result of simple, evolutionary progress – traditional preoccupations provided a historical counterpoint to current concerns in helping to shape it.

Inter-war Indeterminism

The social problems and welfare dilemmas of the twenties and thirties have seemed much more familiar in recent years of economic difficulty than in the golden days of the classic welfare state when they appeared to belong to an alien, lost world. Renewed interest in this period has led to a better appreciation of the extent to which features of later welfare provision, thought to be distinctive, in fact repeated those of earlier years. In eras of comparably scarce resources it is interesting to see both means-testing and concern about welfare 'scroungers.'[1] A similar concern to avoid the political fallout from unpopular changes in welfare provision had the same result, in that a discretionary element was built into benefit regulations in the thirties and seventies.[2] *Ad hoc* growth in social provision also produced the kind of anomalies in benefits – and consequent inequities between recipients – that is criticized today. And we can discern the beginnings of that process whereby the economically better-off obtained more assistance from welfare provision than the deprived for whom it had been intended. In the twenties the skilled worker benefited more from council housing than the unskilled, since only the former could afford the rents, while the lower middle class took up free places in secondary schools with alacrity.

The inter-war years appear indeterminate in the history of social policy as a result of an unstable balance between pressures for inactivity and intervention. The period was dominated by rising unemployment which never fell below a million, and rose to more than three million. Government fears of consequent unrest – or even revolution – were compelling arguments for ameliorative action, but financial orthodoxy, in a period of economic depression, dictated restraint in public expenditure. Economic constraints and Treasury orthodoxy underpinned conservative values and generally tipped the balance towards more 'reactionary' social programmes, since these were usually cheaper. However, this was not invariably the case, and the extension of 'progressive' social insurance – as in the beginning of contributory old-age pensions in 1925 – was seen as more economical than continuation of the unamended non-contributory scheme of 1908. Despite political vacillation and financial restriction, there were significant advances in state welfare provision: notably in the central government assumption of responsibility for 'public' housing in 1919; in the establishment in 1918 of free elementary education and the raising of the school-leaving age from twelve to fourteen; or in the widening of coverage of health and unemployment insurance from a quarter to a half of the adult population. As a result both of these developments, and of greater public expenditure on benefits for the unemployed, the proportion of the gross national product devoted to central and local government expenditure on the social services rose from a pre-war figure of

4 per cent to an inter-war one of 8 per cent.[3] However, it is difficult to see this period either as one of steady and purposeful advance[4] or as one that eventually produced consensus on welfare.[5] Rather, it appears as one of piecemeal, *ad hoc* developments that were unrelated to a wider consensual vision of society and of social welfare. Between 1920 and 1938, for example, there were forty different unemployment insurance acts.

The reconstruction that was planned to follow the First World War exemplified this ambiguity, with tension between the wish for a 'return to normalcy', and a desire to create a new and better world that would be a fitting recompense for the sufferings of war. Although the 'Great War' imposed a brutal intermission in the lifestyle of the privileged, it did not provide an impetus to the kind of radical commitment to social reform that followed the Second World War. On this occasion, the engine of an alleged automatic mechanism linking social reforms to mass participation in war,[6] or to a ratio of military participation,[7] failed to fire efficiently. Part of the differential response may be explained by the varied views of the periods preceding the two wars. Lord Halifax contrasted the situation in 1919 with that facing his audience in 1940: 'We were sure . . . that once we had dealt with the matter in hand the world would return to old ways, which, in the main, we thought to be good ways. You are not so sure.'[8] Indeed, a strong desire to break decisively with the social provision of the inter-war years – the stigma of the Poor Law and the humiliation of the means test – explicitly informed the thinking behind the creation of the classic welfare state between 1945 and 1951. Nevertheless, the marked extension of the state into the economy during 1914–18, the post-war plans of the Ministry of Reconstruction from 1917, and the enhanced self-confidence of bureaucrats in their ability to intervene in complex socio-economic affairs, all pointed towards greater collectivism. And democratic pressures provided potential reinforcement for this, since a stronger impulse for social reform might have followed the trebling of the electorate in 1918. Explanations for the failure of vigorous post-war reform have focused on the weakness of the Ministry of Reconstruction,[9] on the conservative attitudes of government[10] and, most convincingly, on problems of the economy which were so serious that financial orthodoxy cut short any social reform involving large public expenditure. The most conspicuous casualty in this respect was Lloyd George's commitment to build 'homes fit for heroes'. This had found expression in Addison's Housing Act of 1919, only to be halted by 1921 because of what was then seen as the unsupportably high cost of subsidizing council houses.

A more enduring political dilemma over the maximum Treasury contribution permissible for a social policy arose over the extent to which the actuarial basis of the insurance fund could be abandoned. The 1911 insurance scheme for the unemployed had been designed to cope with frictional or modest cyclical unemployment but not the massive structural unemployment of the twenties, and still less the levels of the thirties. As unemployment rose, and the unemployed remained out of work for much longer periods than had been envisaged, so the pressure to adulterate the actuarial basis of the scheme grew. The original provision, whereby length of benefit period was proportional to the record of contributions, was abandoned in 1927. For those whose right to contractual benefit was exhausted, a new status had been devised in 1921 to keep the ordinary worker from the indignity of having to apply for poor relief. This was uncovenanted or extended benefit, known from 1927 as transitional payment. Ironically, although protected from poor-law stigma, those receiving such benefit were subject to a parallel set of humiliations, since similar moral and financial pressures operated. A 'genuinely seeking work' test was begun in 1921 with the intention of preventing 'abuse'; claimants were suspected of being scroungers, and the assumption was one of guilt until proved innocent. It has been estimated that three million claims were disallowed in the period before the test ended in 1930.[11] Since no criteria for the test were ever published, it was effectively one of character, so that disallowance caused enduring bitterness.

The financial crisis of 1931 brought down this dual structure: standard benefit was cut to twenty-six weeks; once this was exhausted those on transitional payment were placed under Public Assistance Committees (PACs). These bodies had come into existence in 1930 as administrative successors to the poor-law guardians and, in popular perception, were little different. Worse, from the point of view of the unemployed, was that their 'benefit' was henceforth not to be of right, but to be subject to a household means test. The impact of this test was severe and, in the first two months of its operation, benefit was reduced or disallowed for half the claimants. During the thirties the government took care to legally define neither the household nor the family and thus made it possible for administrators to extend the number of relatives who were held liable for the support of applicants for assistance.[12] The impact of the means test was thus highly variable: some radical PACs (as in Durham or Rotherham) disregarded virtually all household income in assessing means, while attitudes of local committees elsewhere varied from moderate to stringent. The territorial injustices of the pauper were therefore being perpetuated for the unemployed. And since transitional payments had been financed from 1930 by the Treasury, it was no longer the ratepayer but central government that was picking up a large bill for those who were disregarding its policies. The political unacceptability of this situation led to the creation of the Unemployment Assistance Board (UAB) in 1934, which was to take over assistance to those on transitional payments on the basis of *national* benefit levels, although these were still means-tested. The UAB had also been intended to take unemployment 'outside' politics, through its independent status, regulations and substantial discretionary power. However, its initial benefit levels were inadvertently fixed so low that, on implementation in 1935, they were found to undercut PAC ones in many areas, causing such popular unrest that the board found itself in the eye of a political storm. As a concession to popular feeling, assistance to the unemployed was continued until 1937 at levels that did not undercut pre-existing benefits.

Inter-war relief administration (whether that of the guardians or the PACs) was still informed by traditional moralistic and deterrent values, despite cosmetic changes which converted the workhouse into a poor-law institution in 1913 and abolished the term 'pauper' in 1930. Those localities that wished to initiate a more liberal and humane administration soon found themselves in conflict with central government. First there was the radical challenge of 'Poplarism' in the early twenties, a policy first developed in the east London poor-law union of Poplar, in which generous poor relief was used to safeguard working-class living standards hit hard by large-scale unemployment. This was repeated in less flamboyant style by

Labour-dominated boards of guardians in mining areas in 1926–7, and by some PACs of similar orientation in the early thirties. Since the central authority – the Ministry of Health – did not wish to take over the huge financial responsibility for such relief by transferring it from the local rates to general taxation, full control over local policies was impossible. (A dilemma similar to this has been presented by education in more recent years). For more than a decade the ministry therefore had to resort to a variety of stratagems to deter local independence, notably to civil or financial penalties for targeted local administrators or, in a few extreme cases, to an exemplary central take-over of local bodies. The transfer of the long-term unemployed from the insurance to the assistance sector forced a more radical solution. It was the creation of the UAB in 1934, rather than that of the PACs in 1930, that marked the more decisive break with the Poor Law of a past era. With the transfer of the remaining adult able-bodied males from the PACs to the UAB in 1937, the Poor Law became a residual institution. The fact that it was still responsible for one in forty of the population indicated the transitional character of inter-war welfare, in which the old coexisted uneasily with the new.

There are a number of indicators to suggest that British people during the twenties and thirties experienced some overall improvements in their welfare: health improved, with average life-expectancy up and mortality down; while inter-war surveys found poverty levels dramatically less than those in comparable late-Victorian investigations. But class and regional disparities persisted and, in some cases, worsened. The impact of long-term unemployment on health is a contentious one,[13] but it appears that while the male suffered mainly from psychological problems, his dependants bore the physical brunt of diminished income in malnutrition. This led to problems in pregnancy and childbirth for wives, and to stunted growth for children. Investment in the child was neglected: surveys indicated that poverty was borne disproportionately by children; the health insurance scheme excluded them as dependants from all its benefits; and three out of four pupils quitted school as soon as the statutory leaving age permitted. Women also suffered discrimination: as breadwinners they were penalized in relation to men in the availability and level of health or unemployment benefits they could draw; and as dependants they were excluded, like their children, from health benefits. But both women and children benefited from maternal and child welfare clinics and local authority hospitals, which were part of the burgeoning welfare services of municipalities. Indeed, the multiplicity of overlapping bodies involved in social policy attracted critical comment in 1937 in an authoritative *Report on the British Social Services*, which stated that they had 'grown up in a very piecemeal way, without much regard either for consistency of principle or for the effect of one service on another'.[14] This chaotic situation was to receive radical rationalization in the period that followed.

The Classic Welfare State

On 4 July 1948 the Prime Minister, Clement Attlee, broadcast to the nation. He stated that the social security acts that had come into effect on that day 'are comprehensive and available to every citizen. They give security to all members of the family.' This was a dramatic contrast to the situation a decade earlier, when there was an absence of provision for dependants and selective coverage among breadwinners. In this transformation in welfare from selectivity to comprehensiveness, Attlee might justifiably claim, as he did in 1950, that 'the foundations of the Welfare State have been well and truly laid'.[15] However, this should be seen not just as the achievement of the Labour government after 1945, but also to some extent of the coalition during the preceding war years.

The Second World War was the social catalyst that made the worst features of the 'us and them' or residual welfare unacceptable; it compelled an end to the household means test in 1941. Not only did the war expose deficiencies in welfare; it also created a will to reduce them. Post-war reconstruction plans were seen by the government as a necessary means to maintain civilian morale; initially these had low priority, but popular pressures were sufficiently great to move social reform higher up on the political agenda. The impact of total war on the civilian population was much greater than that of the First World War: such sacrifices were seen by them as requiring recompense, if not reward. Rationing democratized hardship, fostering a greater sense of social cohesion, and bridging – if only for a time –

the divisiveness of an entrenched class system. But the strength of class attitudes and the existence of continuing social divisions should not be underestimated. For example, the evacuation of urban working-class children to rural middle-class homes has usually been seen as forcing an unwelcome realization that 'the submerged tenth described by Charles Booth still exists in our towns like a hidden sore'. But recent research suggests that evacuation probably reinforced class prejudices: the presence of some bed-wetting and lice-ridden child evacuees gave credence to stereotypes of working-class life-styles.[16] The inequities in health and child poverty that were exposed to public scrutiny were sufficiently shocking for action to be taken to lessen the chasm between these continuing Two Nations. This involved greatly extended free 'emergency' medical care, subsidized milk to infants and mothers, and more free milk and meals to children at school. A people's war was thus a somewhat flawed crucible in which was forged a qualified determination to create a people's peace: a 'green and pleasant land' to replace the wastelands of inter-war deprivation.

It is important to appreciate, however, that such resolution was far stronger amongst the electorate and the Labour party than it was amongst most Conservative politicians. That plans for a better Britain were as much a part of the waging of war as they were of post-war reconstruction was a political truth more obvious to the political left than to the right. All sectors of the media proclaimed that a better country could arise from the ashes of the old. Less than a year from the start of hostilities *The Times* had concluded that 'the new order cannot be based on the preservation of privilege'.[17] Public interest in the detail of peacetime social policies was exemplified in a notable issue of *Picture Post* devoted entirely to 'A Plan For Britain'. The editorial stated:

Our plan for a new Britain is not something outside the war, or something *after* the war. It is an essential part of our war aims. It is, indeed, our most positive war aim. The new Britain is the country we are fighting for.[18]

The government quickly responded to popular pressure by appointing a *token* committee of inquiry into social insurance, under a distinguished civil servant – the Liberal, W. H. Beveridge. The cabinet foresaw neither the radicalism of its conclusions, nor the enthusiasm of the public response to the 'Beveridge Report'. Appearing in December 1942, the report became a best-seller. By putting forward a comprehensive programme of social security it articulated, and gave support to, a widespread desire for social reform:

> The prevention of want and the diminution of relief of disease . . . are in fact a common interest of all citizens. It may be possible to secure a keener realization of that fact in war than it is in peace, because war breeds national unity . . . It may be possible through a sense of national unity to bring about changes, which when they are made, will be accepted on all sides as advances.[19]

Receptivity to its recommendations was aided by the mood produced by a great victory at El Alamein in November; a turning-point in war catapulted thoughts forward to peace. 'Action upon the Beveridge Report is an essential war measure . . . [and] a vital prop of the peace structure which must be erected in advance,' stated the *Daily Herald*.[20] The government, under Churchill, failed to gauge the people's mood; afraid of expensive welfare measures, it responded in lukewarm fashion to the report, accepting it in principle but making no detailed commitments. Indeed, the coalition government's published welfare policies were studiously generalized so that they concealed the fundamental differences between the Conservative majority and the Labour minority. The Conservatives saw a future social insurance scheme as essentially a consolidation of inter-war provision with a basis in organized self-help, while their commitment to full employment was qualified by the proviso that this should be consistent with an efficient working of free enterprise.[21] It was predictably the Labour party that had much more radical policies; through skilful parliamentary manoeuvre it became identified in the public mind with Beveridgean welfare reforms. From this time Gallup placed Labour consistently ahead in the polls, until their landslide victory in 1945.

The brightness of the welfare achievements of that Labour ministry of 1945–50 have overshadowed those of the wartime coalition. War accelerated the implementation of reforms that previously had been discussed but not acted upon. However, these radical outcomes can too easily conceal their conservative origin and rationale. Even the epoch-making Beveridge Report, which provided the blueprint for post-war welfare from the cradle to the grave, was to be effected through an extension of an existing principle of social insurance. Beveridge commented that 'the scheme proposed here is in some ways a revolution but in more important ways it is a natural development from the past. It is a British Revolution.'[22] Beveridge's views were both radical and conservative. For example, he had become convinced before the war of the need for family allowances on the ground – stressed by Conservatives – that without them the payment of unemployment benefits sufficiently high to prevent child poverty would erode work-incentives.[23] The values that underpinned the eventual introduction of family allowances in 1945 looked backwards not forwards. Macnicol has argued convincingly that these should be seen rather as a means to perpetuate less eligibility (in the sense we have just outlined) than as an anti-child-poverty measure.[24] Similarly, although Butler's Education Act of 1944 is customarily seen as constituting a massive extension of educational opportunity, its proposals for expanded secondary schooling sprang not so much from egalitarianism as from the social and educational hierarchy recommended in the inter-war Spens and Hadow Reports. Butler himself viewed it as merely 'codifying existing practice'.[25] Thus, as is usually the case, the wartime 'spirit of universalism' had a less heady impact on the work of sober civil servants and politicians than on the expectations of the electorate.

This optimistic mood of the electorate was captured by the Labour manifesto of 1945 with its broad class appeal. Its social and economic policies were rooted in the prescriptions of Beveridge and Keynes. It promised to maintain full employment, introduce a comprehensive system of social security and a National Health Service, and to put into effect the 1944 Education Act. How did the implementation of these policies measure up to the social and economic needs of the British population? In education the school-leaving age was raised to fifteen in 1947, an emergency teacher-training programme instituted, and plans formulated to change secondary-school provision along the lines of the 1944 Act. The rest of the Act fell victim to expenditure cuts dictated by the Treasury, which dominated policy-making. Ironically, this post-war period of excess demand had facilitated a belated conversion to the demand management of

Keynes's *General Theory* by the Treasury, since this merely reinforced the case for cuts in social expenditure. Earlier, much had been made on the hustings by both Labour and Conservative about their house-building plans, since the chief public anxiety (apart from unemployment) was the housing shortage. The Attlee government gave a very high priority to housing: a million permanent houses were built (four-fifths of which were council houses), and a further half million temporary ones were provided. While this fell far short of the commitment, and by no means met the need, it was a solid accomplishment in the face of shortages of materials and curbs on public spending. Indeed, since the importance given to house-building adversely affected capital investment,[26] it arguably retarded future economic growth, so that the resources necessary to underpin welfare schemes in the future were smaller than would otherwise have been the case.

Rapid growth was one of the principal economic objectives of post-war economic policy. There was not a great deal that governments could do to promote more rapid expansion, and a rate of growth that was increasingly seen to be slower than that of her main competitors was widely regarded as a weak feature of Britain's post-war economic performance. In fact, however, output and living standards were expanding more rapidly than at any time since the early nineteenth century, and for a while this contributed to the sense of prosperity which underpinned the first decades of the classic welfare state.

In this context the attainment of full employment was very important. The 1944 White Paper on Employment had committed post-war governments to 'the maintenance of a high and stable level of employment'. The ideas behind this policy had emerged from the debates of the thirties about the adoption of public works programmes as a means of relieving unemployment, and were closely linked to the economic theories and policy proposals of Keynes. It is now clear that many government officials continued to have doubts about the wisdom of such policies, but in the fifties and sixties it was widely believed that the trade cycle had been abolished. The goal of full employment was rapidly achieved and maintained (except for a few weeks of extremely severe weather during February 1947); unemployment among the insured labour force remained at under 2 per cent from 1948 to the end of the Attlee ministry. Indeed, it was not until 1971 that unemployment rose above 3 per cent.

Subsequent analysis has shown that it was buoyant world markets for British exports and a high level of investment by private industry and trade that were primarily responsible for this success.[27] Nevertheless, the belief that governments were committed to full employment and also possessed, in Keynesian policies of demand management, the means to achieve it, probably helped to generate and sustain the confidence required if businessmen were to undertake large-scale programmes of capital investment. This achievement of full employment was perhaps the most obvious contrast to the depressed conditions of the inter-war period. It made a major contribution to the improvements in living standards for the lowest income groups which had suffered most from unemployment, and also accounted for much of the perception of the early post-war decades as a time of rising prosperity.

Unfortunately, however, there was a price to be paid for this. Attempts to restrain the wage inflation that was found to accompany full employment were less than successful. Despite early union moderation, wages rose faster than productivity, and the adverse effect of inflation on lower income groups was causing governmental concern by 1951. There had been apprehension about wage inflation when the policy of full employment had first been formulated. Writing in 1944, for example, Beveridge had feared that making the labour market into a seller's market would

increase permanently and markedly the bargaining strength of labour . . . There is a real danger that sectional wage bargaining, pursued without regard to its effects upon prices, may lead to a vicious spiral of inflation, with money wages chasing prices and without any gain in real wages for the working class as a whole.[28]

However, this dire prophecy was not immediately fulfilled; it was the sixties and seventies that were to feel the full force of this predicament, and the eighties that suffered the adverse effects on social welfare policies that followed from it. In the 1945–51 period, however, the principal gains in living standards – when compared with those of the twenties and thirties – were seen to be derived from full employment. Working-class living standards in these years were also protected by food subsidies, while wartime rates of high income tax were prolonged to help finance the new measures of the welfare state.

The creation of the National Health Service was central to these new measures. Aneurin Bevan, the Minister of Health, commented: 'No society can legitimately call itself civilized if a sick person is denied medical aid through lack of means.'[29] The NHS, by banishing the traditional dread of medical bills, and removing health care from the luxury category, transformed everyday life. It was a tremendous achievement that went well beyond the 1944 White Paper, 'A National Health Service', of the coalition government. This bold creation of a national service in the face of hostile medical vested interests took all Bevan's political skills. He preferred to consult rather than to negotiate with powerful interests, as had his Tory predecessor, Willink. Although Bevan largely reshuffled a pack of existing options his resulting policies were sufficiently radical to progress beyond those in the White Paper of 1944.[30] They involved an extension of the insurance-based panel system to provide a GP service for everyone, as well as the radical restructuring of the patchwork of voluntary and municipal hospitals into a national structure. The first sector of primary medical care was to include dental, ophthalmic and GP services. Bevan eventually outflanked the British Medical Association, which represented the vast majority of GPs, much as Lloyd George had done before him in 1911 at the start of the health insurance scheme. Clinical freedom and free choice of doctor were to be safeguarded. Free health care was extended from the poorer members of society to the entire population, thus reducing the GPs' potential income from private practice. The second part of the tripartite structure involved a nationalization of the hospitals and was the most revolutionary part of the scheme.[31] Specialist care was to be ensured in the state scheme by a trade-off that permitted paybeds and a continuation of private practice for consultants. Finally, there was provision for diverse local authority health and welfare services. When the NHS came into effect in July 1948, the deficiencies of the pre-existing health-care system – so well appreciated by the working class[32] – were immediately exposed. The huge quantity of spectacles and false teeth immediately supplied was a vivid indication of inherited deficiencies in British health care.

July 1948 also saw the start of what the Prime Minister had earlier called a 'wide all-embracing scheme of social insurance designed to give security to the common man'.[33] Based on the Beveridge recommendations, as embodied in the White Paper on Social Insurance of 1944, these policies commanded widespread support. The Beveridge Report had outlined the area that the integrated insurance scheme was to cover:

The term social security is used here to denote the securing of an income to take the place of earnings when they are interrupted by unemployment, sickness, or accident, to provide for retirement through age, to provide against loss of support through the death of another person, and to meet exceptional expenditures . . . Primarily, social security means security of income up to a minimum.[34]

The National Insurance and National Insurance (Industrial Injuries) Acts of 1946 were to fulfil the insurance element, and the National Assistance Act of 1948 provided for extra expenditures. The Minister of National Insurance, James Griffiths, declared with some justice that it was 'the best and cheapest insurance policy offered to the British people, or to people anywhere'.[35] However, the continuance of the principle of flat-rate contributions meant that the level of benefits was also at a low rate. Anxieties that benefits might not achieve subsistence were soon voiced and, as we shall see in the succeeding section, proved to be well founded. In the long term this was to convert the residual safety net of national assistance (later renamed supplementary benefit) into a central rather than a peripheral part of social security.

The enactment of the National Assistance Act in 1948 symbolized the ambiguous character of the classic welfare state. The act stated that 'the existing Poor Law shall cease to have effect', and many Labour MPs were jubilant at what they perceived to be the death-knell of harsh, conditional welfare. 'I think of what we are repealing, more than of what we are proposing,' commented Mrs Braddock.[36] But, in concentrating on changing structures, the importance of continuing social attitudes in perpetuating stigma was ignored by all but a few thoughtful observers. And, for left-wing critics within the Labour party, even the structures had not really been changed; unequal property distribution was unreformed, and egalitarian conference commitments – such as the introduction of comprehensive schools – were ignored. [37] It was also alleged that the 'bourgeois' nature of the period's social welfare measures was evident from their bi-partisan support; seen from this perspective the Attlee reforms represented a minimum previously agreed in principle with the Conservatives. [38]

As well as biases of class, those of gender can also be seen as characteristic of the Beveridgean welfare package. The social security reforms of the forties simultaneously incorporated and marginalized women as had the provisions of the insurance legislation of 1911. In each case the system was organized round the conception of a male labour force so that neither made adequate allowance for the dual reproductive and productive roles of women. In 1911 it had been assumed that it was primarily the male wage that needed to be replaced in times of sickness and unemployment. Even so, the few married women insured under the Act were at the sharp end of inter-war accusations of scrounging and malingering, and consequently suffered from high rates of disallowance in benefit when out of work, and from cutbacks in sickness benefit. A low priority was given to female needs in inter-war discussions on social welfare; the prevailing ideology of maternity and domesticity meant that the woman question was collapsed into a woman-and-child issue that could be met by maternity and infant welfare clinics. Beveridge accepted this traditional view of women as located within the family; his social security provisions reflected a conservative family ideology of female dependency, a male breadwinner, and a family wage. Married women as housewives were therefore to receive their benefits through their husband's insurance. For the minority of married women who did work, the reforms confused insurance with assistance – as contemporary egalitarian feminists alleged – since their lower benefits were justified on the grounds that the husband would provide for their needs. In general the Beveridgean reforms gave first place to marital security and only second place to social security. Yet the history of public assistance indicated the shortcomings of such a view in that – from Victorian poor relief to supplementary benefits – female claimants have outnumbered males. Single, deserted, widowed or divorced mothers have been prominent amongst these women in poverty. These practical deficiencies in Beveridge's idealized view of marriage and mother-hood were compounded by a failure to understand the importance of women's role in the labour force for the income of poorer families. From Booth to Bowley, poverty surveys had already shown that one in three working-class families were dependent, at least par-tially, on female earnings. Post-war trends in the labour market, where labour-force participation by married women has risen steadily, have compounded this misreading of women's domestic role, and consequently exacerbated the distortions within the welfare system. Social policy has thus underwritten female depen-dency within the family, thereby strengthening a distinctive set of male-dominated relationships.[39]

With the passage of time, class and gender biases in the welfare state of the forties have become more visible; most contemporary perceptions were less critical. The Labour manifesto of 1950 sug-gested that Beveridge's vision of 'a comprehensive policy of social progress' had already been achieved. 'Labour has honoured the pledge made in 1945 to make social security the birthright of every citizen. Today destitution has been banished. The best medical care is available to every citizen in the land.'[40]

V

Forty Years on from Beveridge

The four decades since the creation of the classic welfare state have been years of radical changes in political stances towards social welfare but of substantial underlying continuity in its practice. It is this thematic persistence that makes it appropriate to discuss the period as a whole. Of equal significance were hidden deficiencies in the blueprint of social welfare laid down in the Beveridge Report; these became progressively more important, as they were exacerbated during these years by evolving economic circumstances and changing social attitudes. The forties had marked the height of aspiration towards ideals of optimality and universality but the ensuing period ended with a compromised and restrictive model of social welfare. The contrast is starkly apparent in a comparison between the Beveridge Report of 1942 and Fowler's social security reviews of the mid-eighties. Fowler promised that these would constitute 'the most substantial examination of the social security system since the Beveridge Report 40 years ago'.[1] But in place of Beveridge's noble aspirations to banish the five giants of want, idleness, squalor, ignorance and disease, these reviews merely substituted technical adjustments in relationships between subsistence levels, income and welfare benefits. And where Beveridge had produced popular enthusiasm Fowler provoked disagreement.

These forty years of social policy fall into two roughly equal but contrasting parts. The fifties were halcyon years. Complacency that the welfare state had been achieved was disturbed only by issues in the National Health Service. (Amongst them was a furore over the introduction of charges for teeth and spectacles, allegations of extravagance, and anxiety over the relationship between finite resources and rising demands.) This period of optimism ended in the mid-sixties with the twin discovery that substantial numbers living on state benefits were in poverty, and that many were not claiming benefits for which they were eligible. Problems continued to be identified within the framework of the Beveridge Report, and the public remained confident that if needs were identified, then remedial action would be taken. That the welfare state should have these expanding frontiers was the common currency of almost all social policy discussion at that time. The rediscovery of poverty or, more accurately, its redefinition as inequality by social scientists on the political left, provided a stick with which to beat the Labour ministries of 1964–70, and to press for more generous provision of benefits. But the sterling crisis of 1966, and the devaluation of the following year, gave an indication to the more clearsighted that further progress was dependent not so much on social aspiration as upon economic growth, since this had provided a relatively painless means of financing expanding welfare provision.

Cost constraints assumed greater importance in the seventies and eighties, and with them came some recognition that priorities and selectivity must have a strategic role in social policy. The nature of the bi-partisan consensus on the welfare state became more contentious at this time, less in terms of the policies pursued in social policy (on which most contemporary comment focused) than in the place that welfare occupied in a wider spectrum of policies. While in office both Labour and the Conservatives followed similar social security policies of means-testing, and increasingly departed from the earlier ideal of universality. But whereas the former saw this as a forced compromising of social ideals, the latter viewed it as desirable containment of state welfare. The right also pointed to failures in public provision, notably in housing, and considered the market a more efficient mechanism to meet such needs. Also present in right-wing thinking were fiscal and occupational welfare systems that were seen as having important complementary roles to state welfare. With the election of successive Thatcher governments after 1979, the 'Butskellite' consensus on welfare ended. It became apparent that the long-term objective was to replace what still remained of the universality of the classic welfare state by 'state welfare' of a more residual kind. Basic state benefits were to be targeted on those who needed them most, while others were to be persuaded to supplement or replace public with private welfare provision.

From a long-term perspective such a redrawing of the boundary between collectivism and individualism forms only one of a historical series, involving a shifting division between individual and social responsibilities. The eighties then have a less apocalyptic character than that given by much contemporary comment written within a much shorter time horizon. Viewed like this the balance of responsibility laid down in the classic welfare state appears as only one of a number of possible democratic positions. And the close relationship between restrictionist social policies and economic depression in the post-1973 period also seems less unexpected when set against comparable experiences in the 1830s or 1920s and 1930s. Less predictable, perhaps, was the way in which, by the late sixties, the welfare state had been imbued with moral virtues of fairness, integration, social citizenship and egalitarianism. This encouraged expectations that were easier to meet from expanding resources in more prosperous early years than from redistribution in later lean ones. By the seventies the incompatibility of some of the original objectives of the classic welfare state was also becoming apparent; full employment without union wage-restraint bred inflation that endangered the economic growth on which other social policy objectives depended. And, in rejecting some of those original aims – in preferring to cut inflation, at the cost of raising unemployment to unprecedented heights in the early eighties – the early Thatcher governments found that a rising benefits bill for the unemployed and their families blunted their attempt to restrict the frontiers of the welfare state. By the mid-eighties those who in earlier years would have been highly critical of slow progress in the attainment of expanding welfare objectives were busily defending the ramparts of existing provision, lest it shrink still more. Further attacks from the New Right on what was still seen as swollen collectivism indicated possible further cuts in welfare. Outside those ramparts, Marxists drew new strength for their critique of welfare capitalism from the expansion of fiscal and occupational welfare (reviewed in Chapter VI), and feminists found new ammunition with which to assail the patriarchal character of welfare provision. The limited consensus on social welfare of the early post-war period had been replaced by increasingly polarized and acrimonious debate.[2]

Social Security after Beveridge

The Beveridge Report had advocated 'social insurance for basic needs; national assistance for special cases'.[3] While lip-service has been paid to this as a basic principle of social policy, changes in society and the economy have rapidly made its practical implementation obsolescent. As a result, much recent development in social security has been concerned with the results of inadequate insurance provision for basic needs, and with the consequent growth of supplementary assistance. This has undercut another of the report's principles, that there should be 'adequacy of benefit in amount and time. The flat rate of benefit proposed is intended in itself to be sufficient without further resources to provide the minimum income needed for subsistence in all normal cases.'[4] And in the subsequent growth of graduated insurance contributions (notably in pensions), there has been a departure from Beveridge's conception of citizenship linked to benefits as of right. In his view this presupposed that 'all insured persons, rich and poor, will pay the same contributions for the same security'.[5] Universality of contributions and benefits would, it was widely assumed, destroy the sense of stigma associated with residual welfare. This was to prove over-optimistic. 'Forty years on' from Beveridge we can see that – like the heroes of the song of that name – age has diminished the body of principles, enhancing by contrast a past golden age when youthful vigour reigned.

Let us evaluate departures from Beveridge's blueprint, looking at the overall significance of what occurred, and the reasons for it. This historical overview will concentrate on major developments in order to reduce the complexity that makes informed discussion of more fundamental issues difficult. Three issues were dominant in debate during these forty years: the meaning and extent of poverty; the respective merits of universal and selective benefits; and the relative levels of benefits and of wages in relation to the maintenance of work-incentives.

We begin by looking at the relationship between assistance and insurance. The Beveridge Report had argued that 'social insurance should be comprehensive, in respect both of the persons covered, and of their needs'.[6] The National Assistance Board (created in 1948) was thus intended only as a welfare safety net – of last rather than first resort. 'Social insurance should aim at guaranteeing the minimum income needed for subsistence.'[7] However, insurance payments from the very beginning fell below subsistence levels, so that recourse was necessary to assistance for needs that – according to Beveridge's blueprint – should have been met by insurance. At the end of 1948 nearly one million people were receiving national assistance, in 1966 the figure was two million, and by the early eighties it was more than four million. The extent of the short-fall in insurance payments as a guarantee of subsistence had also worsened: two-thirds of the households being assisted in 1948 were receiving insurance benefits, while by the mid-sixties all but a small minority were in receipt of insurance-based benefits.[8] Beveridge's expectation that 'the scope of assistance will be narrowed from the beginning and will diminish'[9] was falsified by an increasingly circumscribed coverage of needs by national insurance.

The national minimum standard of life envisaged by Beveridge was austere, being based on a modification of Rowntree's poverty line in 1938 as used in his second poverty survey of York. But the benefits of 1948 only compensated for two-fifths of the inflation that had occurred since 1938. Even so, Rowntree's third survey of York in 1950 *appeared* to show that poverty was declining; only 3 per cent of the working class were in poverty, whereas without the welfare measures of the forties this would have been 22 per cent. Accordingly, there was little awareness that the welfare state was failing to meet needs during the fifties, as was actually the case.[10] In the sixties the discovery of a large extent of pensioner poverty caused concern. That half of the households receiving national assistance were those of pensioners in 1948 was only part of the problem since, by 1965, the government itself concluded that nearly one-third of pensioners entitled to benefit were not claiming it.[11] This problem of low take-up became a more general problem as assistance became increasingly a matter of benefits subjected to unpopular, individual means tests.

In 1948 there had been only three individually means-tested benefits: non-contributory pensions (i.e. those begun in 1908); school meals; and national assistance. At that date, two million people – or about one in twenty-four of the British population –

were dependent on them. By 1982, however, one in eight people received means-tested benefits, or as many as one in four if means-tested rate rebates were also included.[12] That means-testing emerged as part of the welfare state was a result of a bi-partisan consensus that stemmed from very different reasoning. Labour saw it as an undesirable setback to universalist ideals; an unwelcome consequence of inflation and economic stringency. The Conservatives, by contrast, tended to see it in a more favourable light, as a way to preserve work-incentives within a more minimalist framework of social welfare. Because of the legacy of intense bitterness over the inter-war household means test, the existence of an individual means test in what purported to be a new era was viewed with popular dislike. 'In no country is the means test, as a condition of social aid, so widely resented as in Britain,' commented *The Times* in 1952.[13]

Recognition of the defects of the scheme of assistance, as laid down in 1948, came eighteen years later with a new system that was intended

to remove features which tended to discourage some people from claiming, and to make the system easier for people to understand and fairer as between one person and another . . . [and to] encourage as many as possible of those who might be entitled to benefit to claim it.[14]

It had been found that pensioners had been refraining from claiming for a variety of reasons: notably ignorance on the one hand, and pride – with dislike of charity or assistance – on the other. The replacement of national assistance by supplementary benefits in 1966 involved an emphasis on benefits as of right and an intended change of ethos in their administration. Despite this, and some notable campaigns during the seventies to increase the public's awareness of their welfare rights, take-up of an expanded array of means-tested benefits remained low. At the end of the seventies academic studies suggested that take-up rates for the principal means-tested benefits were in the range from one-half to four-fifths of entitlement.[15] Since then there has been some improvement, although the unemployed still have a very high rate of unclaimed entitlements.[16]

'We are now taxing the poor to help the poor,' exclaimed the Meacher Committee of the House of Commons in 1983,[17] expressing a sentiment that would have been all too familiar to a critic of the

Victorian system of poor rates. But because of a recent extension of income-related benefits, the problem has been compounded. 'Poor' people are now seen as sufficiently rich to be taxed, while at the same time they are seen as sufficiently poor to be assisted. Inflation has meant that even those slightly above the poverty line assumed in supplementary benefits now pay income tax. The combination of low tax thresholds, with means-tested benefits possessing a steep rate of withdrawal as income rises, has resulted in a poverty trap for many low-income families. This means that low-income workers may lose all or most of any increase in earnings, because they then pay more in income tax and national insurance but, at the same time, have means-tested benefits withdrawn. A related but rather different problem – that of very low earnings – had earlier led to the introduction of the 'wage-stop'. This rule was grounded in the anxiety that, if benefits for a wage earner and dependants were higher than wages, work-incentives would suffer. As a result, if an individual earned less in work than the level of supplementary benefits, payment of benefit was kept below the wage level. But, since the supplementary benefit payment was at a broadly subsistence level, this then perpetuated family poverty. It was the wage-stop – operative from 1966 to 1975 – that most clearly illustrated the continued vitality of the Victorian concept of less eligibility in the modern period.

The poverty trap has affected more people as the range of means-tested benefits has grown. Although the rhetoric of political disagreement between the political parties over these benefits has at times been intense, there has been substantial continuity in actual policy between the parties while in office. Since the mid-seventies there has been an increased recognition of the constraints that finite economic resources impose on social policy. In turn, this has led to a greater acceptance of the inevitability of means-testing as a way of concentrating benefits where need is greatest. And an expansion of such testing appears to be the logic of the transition from an absolute poverty line (defined in narrowly materialistic subsistence terms, as in Rowntree's primary poverty line) to a more relative standard (defined as a percentage of average standards of living or by cultural norms). The supplementary benefits level is relativistic in a limited sense, because it is influenced by changing standards of living in its allowances for expenditure.

Since the late sixties the subject of means-testing has provoked a vigorous and only partially resolved discussion involving a number of important related questions and responses. First, were means-tested benefits the appropriate way to ensure that scarce resources went to those whose need was greatest? This was central to the 'selectivity versus universality' debate, waged fiercely since the sixties, where many have now conceded to the selectivists. Second, did means-tested benefits – precisely because they were selectively targeted – necessarily involve a sense of stigma, and a resulting low take-up? The perpetuation of older social attitudes to welfare has increasingly been recognized as an intractable problem, and one that is resistant to easy solutions such as a change in administrative mechanisms and nomenclature (as occurred in 1966 from assistance to benefits). The Poor Law legally died in 1948 but is socially still alive in attitudes that stigmatize certain forms of welfare. Third, could means-tested benefits avoid very high marginal tax rates that result in a poverty trap for recipients? Purported solutions in the form of a negative income tax or social dividend have served largely to perpetuate civil war among social-policy analysts rather than to achieve consensual remedies. Fourth, could flexibility in response to need be reconciled with claimants' desire to know their welfare rights? Bureaucratic responses in recent years have ricocheted back and forth between equally undesirable extremes of rigid rules or administrative discretion. This has made it appear as if individual injustices and social waste were an inevitable consequence of extending selective assistance into a major role in social welfare. Finally, how were work-incentives to be maintained when some family breadwinners earned an income so low that it was much the same as that paid out as subsistence benefit? While there is recognition – as indeed there has been since the thirties – that some form of child allowance or credit was the best way to prevent family poverty, there appears to be continued social and political reluctance to implement adequate benefits of this nature.

Figure 1 indicates that the social security sector within public social expenditure has been the most costly in the post-war period, and also that its outlays have risen particularly rapidly from the mid-seventies. Looked at from the claimants' point of view, however, the achievement of social security has been only a qualified success. Over the period 1948–84, supplementary benefit levels for short-term claimants have maintained their value as a proportion of average male manual earnings, while for long-term claimants the real value of benefits, so defined, has improved slightly.[18] But since manual workers are a declining proportion of the workforce, this suggests that the living standards of people on welfare have not reflected those of an increasingly affluent society. One cause of continuing poverty has been the flat rate of national insurance contributions on which Beveridge had laid so much stress. In 1981 poverty afflicted more than one in four people, and nearly one in three families. (Poverty is here defined according to the widely accepted standard of 140 per cent of the supplementary benefit level.)

The existence of poverty in families (particularly those of the unemployed, or those headed by a single parent) has become the main focus of social concern in the eighties, as pensioner poverty had been in the early sixties. This appreciation of the changing shape of the poverty problem has encouraged an incremental approach to social security. Earlier Utopian hopes that poverty might be abolished through the agency of the welfare state have been replaced by more restricted aims. An increased understanding of the multiple causes of social deprivation, and hence of its intractability, has sobered expectations.[19] So too has an appreciation of 'diswelfare', or the problems that social policies – and the welfare agencies that implement them – inadvertently cause for clients. And the reluctance of taxpayers to finance more than very small redistributive social policies suggests the limitations of egalitarian policies in an inegalitarian society. The attempt by the Thatcher governments to reinforce work-incentives by widening the wage/benefit ratio, both through raising tax thresholds and by abolishing earnings-related unemployment benefit, has indicated a more restricted future role for welfare. Electoral successes by the New Right have effectively given popular endorsement to more circumscribed aims for social security since 1979. This has provoked fears of residual welfare and less well-founded anxieties that there will emerge an underclass of permanent recipients of welfare.

Figure 1: Social Expenditure as Percentage of GDP in the UK, 1951–85

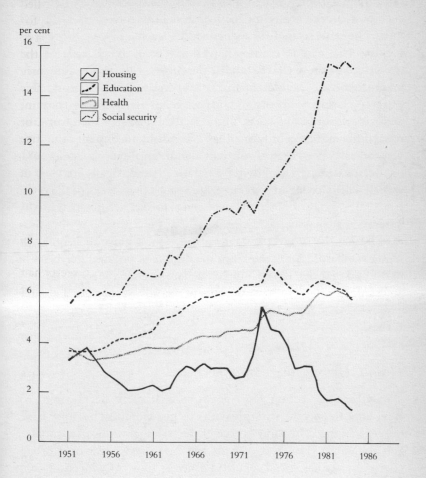

Source: National Income and Expenditure (Central Statistical Office)

Evaluating the welfare achievements in social security provision during the last forty years, in relation to the continued existence of such pronounced economic inequalities in our society, is a difficult task. The criteria used for assessment in such a discussion remain controversial. Some commentators have effectively replaced the objectives of the welfare state of the forties with those stemming from socialistic egalitarianism, and a relativistic conception of poverty. Using a historical perspective, it is clear that some of Beveridge's formative ideas on the welfare state stemmed from the quite different tenets of Edwardian Liberalism; the input of the state was to be balanced against substantial individual action in determining personal welfare and living standards. Paradoxically, in view of the left's defence of '*the*' welfare state against the attacks of the New Right, Beveridge might well have been in greater sympathy with the latter over such issues as the importance of incentives, or of individual (rather than collectivist) determination of more than minimal living standards. And seen from the dominant political perspective of the mid-eighties, the egalitarian welfare ideals of the sixties seem – at least for a time – to have become practically obsolete to a greater extent than the more limited ones of the classic welfare state of the forties.

Health, Housing and Education

The preceding section has suggested that forty years after the Beveridge Report the struggle with the 'giant' of want has now gone into extra time. The same is true of the war against disease, squalor and ignorance. Policies towards the NHS have shown a broad continuity, as has social security, whereas those of education, and still more of housing, have displayed abrupt changes arising from political disagreements.

The National Health Service Act of 1946 had aimed to establish 'a comprehensive health service designed to secure improvement in the physical and mental health of the people of England and Wales and the prevention, diagnosis and treatment of illness'.[20] Thirty-three years later, the Royal Commission on the Health Service hinted at the difficulties of implementing them; problems of availability and maldistribution of resources in the face of rising consumer expectations and demands. It described the aims of the NHS as being to

encourage and assist individuals to remain healthy; provide equality of entitlement to health services; provide a broad range of services of a high standard; provide equality of access to these services; provide a service free at the time of use; satisfy the reasonable expectations of its users; remain a national service responsive to local needs.[21]

Such generality itself suggests why popular expectations caused continued problems. What was a 'reasonable' expectation of health and did this include transplants, hip replacements or remodelled noses on demand? The basic problem was that health service *resources* remained finite, whilst over the years *demand* expanded way beyond what had originally been foreseen. (This might have been expected, given a comparable experience after the 1911 Insurance Act, when there had been a steadily increasing use of the new panel doctors.[22]) Patients' expectations of the NHS had escalated as a result both of a redefinition of what 'health' meant within a more affluent society, and of what could be achieved by vastly improved medical technology and pharmaceuticals. Better health care in the NHS, with improved standards of living, helped people to live longer; the longer they lived the more health care they needed. Rising demand was, in a fundamental sense, internally self-sustaining as well as being fed by external pressures. Figure 1 indicates the steadily rising proportion of UK resources that have been devoted to health, of which public expenditure on the NHS took the lion's share.

At the same time, there was increasing awareness of continued inequality in the resources available to meet demand. Local distribution of GPs, and regional availability of hospital beds, was uneven at the inception of the NHS, and redistribution proceeded very slowly. And, just as there were regions starved of resources, so, historically, there were 'Cinderella' services – those for the mentally ill, mentally handicapped and geriatric patients – which, in the allocation of resources, had done worse than 'high tech', acute medicine. Even when Cinderella was eventually chosen to go to the NHS Ball, it proved difficult to allocate extra resources to allow her to do so in style. The Royal Commission on the NHS recognized in 1979 that only 1 per cent extra funding could in practice go to the new priority sectors of the elderly, the mentally ill, the handicapped, and children. These inequities in provision, within a national service, were matched by marked differences in morbidity and mortality between social classes. Indeed, in 1980 the Black Report's controversial conclusions suggested that class differentiation in health had actually *increased* during the period of the NHS.[23] These continued inequities fundamentally challenged the objective of national provision within a democratic society.

It was vital that public and political support for a comprehensive health service should continue, enabling the NHS to be financed through general taxation, since three-fifths of NHS expenditure went on patients who were 'bad risks', and were unlikely to be able to afford to pay for health care through insurance. A rising proportion of the money for the NHS has been derived from general taxation; from around 70 per cent in the forties to 85 per cent by the mid-eighties. Although much was made about the very existence – or the precise level – of prescription charges, their *financial* importance over the years has been exaggerated. In part this is because even by 1985/6 – after a period of very rapid increases – less than 5 per cent of NHS finance came from this source. Also important was that a rising number of exemptions has meant that a declining number of patients actually paid such prescription charges. Politically, of course, in the earlier days of the NHS, charges were perceived to impede access to its central benefit – *free* health care at the point of entry. This feature appeared to the British people to be its principal glory, and so recurrent debates over prescription charges (imposed in 1951, removed in 1965, and reimposed in 1968) had a symbolic resonance quite disproportionate to the actual sums involved.

Turning now from NHS income to that of expenditure, restricted budgets but increased demand for health services have meant that the issue of priorities has had to be confronted. In the sixties this focused on the building programme and the urgent need to replace old hospitals (principally those inherited from the Poor Law), and meant that the NHS had to fight for extra resources against other demands for improved welfare services. After 1976, the issue was internal to the NHS, and involved a redistribution of resources through the application of the RAWP (Resources Allocation Working Party) formula. This attempted – with qualified success – to benefit deprived regions of the health service (mainly in the north) at the expense of the historically better-funded London and south-eastern region. It did nothing, however, to redress inequalities *within* regions.

Patients were not troubled by such invisible abstractions but, by the seventies, they were increasingly concerned about the queues for hospital operations that were a visible sign of the kinds of problem that such technocratic solutions were designed to meet. Queues were effectively a rationing device and reflected the NHS's financial inability to meet expanding demand. Restricted budgets in the face of such apparently endless escalation led to a preoccupation with the reorganization of structures and the enhancement of efficiency, in order to reduce duplication, maldistribution and waste. Major administrative upheavals in 1974, 1982 and 1984 were intended to integrate the NHS more effectively and to increase managerial efficiency – especially in hospitals, where 70 per cent of NHS expenditure is incurred. These were soon followed by an era of 'efficiency savings'; reduced spending that was intended to follow the contracting out of NHS ancillary services. Hope of financial saving has been an important – if concealed – reason for a recent switch to community care for former patients in mental institutions. These savings have proved to be illusory but the movement has exposed the lack of integration in the administration and financing of community and hospital services within the NHS. To remedy this situation the Griffiths Report recommended in 1988 that local authorities should in future take over the main responsibility for community care.

In the third sector of the health service, earlier improvements in the organizational effectiveness of primary care were to prove more successful. They transformed general practice from a predominantly single-handed enterprise to a group activity; by 1981, three out of four family doctors had joined a group practice, and one out of four was attached to a health centre. Overall, these organizational changes have led to a more informed and continuous provision of care by GPs for their patients and, in the hospital sector, to some shortening of queues for non-urgent operations through a more efficient use of bed-space and of medical personnel. In the future, a more cost-effective health service for patients will involve greater emphasis on preventive measures as well as difficult choices about who should get which treatment. Whether doctors or health economists are cast in the role of God, this will necessitate an analysis of output rather than – as in the past – a focus on input.

Past medical, economic and administrative priorities have not necessarily been those that patients or the community might have chosen. Criticism of 'welfare constituencies' in the NHS has usually focused on the influence wielded by ancillary staff in resisting 'efficiency savings'. This was not unimportant but, with more justice, criticism might also focus on the responsibility that the medical profession bears for the perpetuation of a remarkably uneven distribution of resources within the health service, both in terms of specialism and of region (in effect, of class). Those in long queues for conditions termed by others as 'non-urgent' have not been well served by the allocation of large sums of money to body-scanners or transplant surgery that would be of benefit to much smaller numbers of patients. Even worse has been the fate of those trapped in a limbo between past institutional treatment and future community provision. And the low priority accorded to prevention rather than to treatment on the one hand, and reluctance to employ para-medical staff rather than doctors on the other, has meant a perpetuation of high- rather than low-cost measures to improve health in the community.

The NHS was planned as a *national* service by its architect, Aneurin Bevan and, at its inception, nearly all joined it. In comparison with the inter-war panel system the NHS soon offered patients primary care with better doctor/patient ratios and slightly longer consultation periods, treatment in improved surgery accommodation with more up-to-date equipment, and opportunities for easy referral to more specialist consultant and hospital care. Its actual *record* of achievement has been generally sound in that it has made more efficient use of limited resources, as shown for example by faster 'through-put' of hospital patients, or increased expenditure on 'units of need', as defined by different age groups of patients treated in hospital and community services. But the record has not proved sufficiently good for it to achieve a truly national (i.e. uniform) service. Perhaps, inevitably, it has also failed to match increased *expectations* that have been generated in part by comparisons with provision in more affluent nations. This has contributed to an upward but fluctuating trend in the number of patients opting for private health insurance. Whereas only 50,000 had done so at its inception, by the end of 1987 5.7 million people were covered by private insurance.[24]

The *perception* that the state was in certain respects offering a second-class service was evident in the educational field as well, where a number of middle-class consumers also left the state sector and 'went private'. In housing, however, the market was always of greater importance and private builders have met a major part of the housing need. This has been underpinned by massive tax subsidies to private house-owners through the fiscal welfare state, whereas council housing has been financed through the classic welfare state.

Housing has been a politically divisive issue in a way that the NHS has never been, and policy bias has been based in electoral rationale. Labour has consistently tried to increase the stock of council housing, while the Conservatives have given higher priority to expanding owner-occupation. In 1946 Bevan set the agenda for Labour ministries when he stated as Housing Minister that 'we propose to start to solve, first, the housing difficulties of the lower income groups'. The Conservative government's White Paper on Housing of 1961 provided the rival political philosophy on housing when it commented that, 'As real incomes go up, more and more of this [housing] need . . . should be met by private enterprise.' In the immediate post-war era each party out-bid the other in ambitious plans to end the housing shortage, and in the early fifties the Conservatives continued Labour's priority of council over private housing. After 1954, however, they attempted to channel local authority (council) housing to meet specific needs in providing for old people, and rehousing inhabitants of slum or overcrowded accommodation. They also ended licensing of private building, thus freeing resources. A greater proportion of private houses relative to council houses was therefore built under the Conservatives from 1954 to 1964. This relative balance of construction continued thereafter under Labour, but was the inadvertent result of the 1967 devaluation on public expenditure programmes; hence the cut-back that council housing thereafter suffered. After 1970, and again after 1979, the annual totals of council housing completed declined as a result of policy priorities by the governments of Heath (1970–4) and Thatcher (after 1979). Totals for the Labour government of 1974–9 initially increased but, like its predecessor of 1964–70, severe external financial pressures on public expenditure plans led to later cutbacks. Over the years, the council housing provided by local authorities has proved to be much more vulnerable to the cumulative impact of government spending cuts than any other area of welfare. These recent battles between central and local authorities over housing have their antecedents in inter-war conflicts over public assistance; in each case central government paid the piper and called the tune.

Growth in overall accommodation has been such that by the mid-seventies fit housing stock was said to exceed the number of households and there was – in theory at least – a housing surplus. And, despite the creation of what were effectively new slums in the high-rise council blocks of the sixties, the overall standard of housing had considerably improved. The character of the housing market had also altered dramatically. The private rented housing market appeared to be in near-terminal decline. This was the end-product of a long-term process in which capital appreciation in the value of houses, when set besides rents subject to increased control, made sale more attractive to private landlords than rental. A free market had disappeared with the first imposition of rent controls in 1915, and had never since come near to being restored.[25] Legislative changes in the fifties and sixties drastically curtailed the private rented sector. The introduction of 'fair rents' and the protection of sitting tenants by the Rent Act of 1965 sought to protect tenants from the 'Rachmanism' of huge rent increases and evictions that had followed the de-control of rents in 1957. But the private landlord then found that he was effectively subsidizing the tenant, and this made private rentals uneconomic from the landlord's point of view. Between 1951 and 1981, private rented housing declined from 52 to 12 per cent of the housing stock in England and Wales. Within the same period, owner-occupation increased from 31 to 57 per cent of the total, and public-sector housing rose from 17 to 31 per cent.[26]

What was the significance of this expanded council-house sector? It meant that low-income families could live in decent housing which was subsidized. At first the subsidy was general but, since

1972, that subsidy changed to a more economical one, based on the means-testing of individual incomes of tenants. Not all who have wanted council accommodation have been eligible, or able, to rent it. Growing waiting-lists have led to the adoption of more complex allocation procedures (in terms of a points system based on perception of need), rather than that of simply waiting to reach the head of the queue. This has benefited some and penalized others. Such inequity is likely to worsen as a result of a severe squeeze on local authorities; the annual total of council houses built has been cut by 80 per cent between 1979 and 1987.[27] The severity of these cut-backs can be seen in Figure 1, which shows a steep fall in public expenditure on housing after the mid-seventies. The Housing Act of 1980 has also diminished the size of the public rented sector. This was a revolutionary – and, at first, a politically very contentious – change in policy which, for the first time, permitted council-house tenants to purchase their homes on very advantageous terms. By 1988 it had led to one million sales, mainly those of higher quality. And, since it was the better part of the stock of council housing that was transferred into private hands, local authority accommodation seemed to be becoming a residual sector.

By the mid-eighties, Britain had a more socially divided housing provision than any other European country, with the lower income groups in rented council housing, and the more affluent housed in their own property. (The impact of housing associations – funded through government money but providing privately rented accommodation – has so far bridged this gap to only a very limited extent.) Since 1979 owner-occupation has expanded rapidly so that by 1987 it amounted to nearly two-thirds of the total. A powerful reason for this has been that owner-occupiers enjoy a form of subsidy from the Exchequer (through tax relief on mortgage interest payments) that is much greater than that given to council-house tenants. An increasingly complex and chaotic structure of housing subsidies of various kinds frequently channels assistance away from those whose need is greatest. A dual tradition of council housing and owner-occupation, both subsidized through the state but through different mechanisms, has produced an anomalous situation: a 'property-owning democracy' of increasingly segregated and inequitable housing provision.

In the field of education the trend has been quite the opposite in that – at least until the late eighties – school provision had been made less hierarchical and more comprehensive in nature. The major change had been that from the tripartite secondary school system (established under the 1944 Act) to one of comprehensives. Debates about the social injustices perpetuated in the 11-plus examination, which selected eleven-year-old children to secondary schools of different types, were central to the aspirations of those aiming to extend the welfare state. The objectives of the Department of Education's circular 10/65, in seeking to accelerate the trend from the divisive system of secondary moderns and grammar schools to the social inclusiveness of the comprehensive, marked a high point in egalitarianism in 1965. Equality of opportunity in education would, it was thought by many, help create a less class-ridden society. Together with the expansion in university places (proposed in the Robbins Report of 1963), it would provide a ladder of meritocratic opportunity for the individual. Expanded resources for education also appeared self-evidently beneficial to society at large. Economic growth was viewed as dependent on educational investment, and this economic growth would then facilitate further progress in other welfare programmes. Hope of social engineering and optimism about the potentiality of the welfare state were mutually reinforcing. The enhanced role of academics as social policy experts and informal government advisers at this time powerfully reinforced these circular flows of social and educational optimism.

After 1973 this educational euphoria was dissipated; economic pressures and the end of bi-partisan agreement on education meant that first one and then another institution was affected by cuts. Figure 1 shows the extent of the fall in educational expenditures from the mid-seventies onwards. Demographic predictions of falling birth-rates led to restrictions in resources for teacher-education, then primary and secondary schools, and finally further and higher education. Shrinking sectors encouraged administrators to initiate successive waves of institutional reorganization. Economic problems intensified educational difficulties; not only did inflation erode real resources but the faltering British economy apparently falsified the linkage between educational investment and economic growth. And the ideological sea-change of the seventies encouraged right-wing attacks on the educational and social achievements of institutions reformed in the sixties. The comprehensives were said to be neglecting their more able pupils; those primary schools that had adopted innovations praised in the Plowden Report of 1967 were pilloried for preferring social objectives to the attainment of numeracy and literacy; and colleges of education were accused of filling the heads of prospective teachers with irrelevant educational theory. But criticisms were not merely the preserve of the political right. The Labour Prime Minister James Callaghan initiated the 'Great Debate' on educational standards in 1976, which has had as its lineal descendant the proposals for a national curriculum in the Education Reform Act of 1988. By the eighties the targets for criticism had become even more widespread. Universities were alleged to be extravagant and inefficient in that their output was said by government to give a poor return on the money invested in them. Both the universities and the research councils (which fund academic research) were exhorted to look not to the state but to the market for some of their resources, as well as for their efficiency models.

The result of these changes has been to lower morale and to produce a defensive posture by educationalists towards the further changes proposed for the late eighties and beyond. Yet in terms of the very considerable achievements of the state educational sector since the fifties this has not been altogether appropriate. The postwar baby boom had meant that the system had to cope with much larger numbers and did so while raising standards in a number of ways. The main egalitarian achievement of state education has been in younger age groups; in the better deal given to working-class pupils through a longer secondary schooling (arising from the raising of the school-leaving age to sixteen in 1973); and in greater opportunities for less academic pupils to take external examinations. But the proportion of the age group staying on at school or college voluntarily, or going on to higher or further education after the age of eighteen, is still conspicuously lower than in comparable countries. There has been a notable improvement in the proportion of women proceeding to universities but not in numbers of working class students. Overall, however, middle-class children have been the greatest beneficiaries of the expanded role of the state in education, through their disproportionately high take-up of education after the age of 16. The middle class has also been prominent in its gains from other states of welfare – notably the fiscal and occupational welfare discussed in the following chapter.

VI

Other States of Welfare

The role of the state in social affairs has fluctuated considerably over time. In our period the history of public welfare (collectivist activity popularly understood as *the* welfare state) needs to be set alongside that of private welfare (voluntary activity of a philanthropic or charitable nature). It should also be placed in the context of other forms of state welfare. It was Richard Titmuss, in a now-famous lecture of 1955, 'The Social Division of Welfare', who drew attention to the fact that concentrating solely on state welfare missed two-thirds of the story – fiscal and occupational welfare: 'At present these three systems are seen to operate as virtually distinct systems.'[1] For reasons that are discussed later, not all would agree that fiscal and occupational welfare should be regarded as components in an analysis of welfare. Others would not only accept this tripartite division but extend it further, and argue that a complex mixed system of welfare is in operation: informal as well as formal, and private as well as public. The multiplicity of sources of present-day welfare appears to have taken some social policy specialists by surprise. However, a longer time perspective than that of the last forty years (the period most commonly employed) should have suggested that social welfare has always been mixed, with different sectors of social welfare delivering similar services. What perhaps is novel is that certain states of welfare, particularly that given informally in the family and the community – are today achieving greater public visibility and political significance.

Voluntaryism

In the nineteenth century, the voluntary sector was in a very real sense the foundation of social welfare, but gradual appreciation of its inadequacies in meeting the rapidly growing needs of a larger, industrialized, urban population was instrumental in the growth of supplementary or alternative services by public agencies. By the mid-twentieth century, growth in this collectivist provision had in turn made public welfare appear central, and private welfare subsidiary. Only in the last few years – with rhetoric on rolling back the frontiers of the (public) welfare state – has there been a revived interest in voluntaryism. In the eighties its most enthusiastic British advocates see its future as very much more than that of the junior partner in social policy provision. Viewed from this longer time-perspective, Beveridge's view that voluntary agencies should do 'those things which the state should not do' appears ahistorical.[2] T. H. Marshall was more perceptive in his view that 'there is no clear case for assigning some areas wholly to one and some wholly to the other'.[3]

Discussion over the division between public and private welfare has been concerned not only with financial issues (who pays), but also with moral questions (who should benefit). In nineteenth-century debate moral issues were raised more explicitly, although recent references to the fostering of 'community spirit' through voluntaryism suggest that a moral dimension is still implicit in modern discussion. During the Victorian era it was axiomatic that private charity was morally superior to public relief from the Poor Law. It was believed that exchanging the fruits of such private benevolence strengthened ties between the propertied and the poor, and elevated both donor and recipient. Ideally, it was thought that the recipient should be worthy of such charity. And, since poverty was often interpreted as frequently being the result of moral failure, it followed that the 'undeserving' or feckless poor should be relegated to the Poor Law, and that charitable assistance should be directed at the 'deserving' or respectable poor who had become impoverished through circumstances beyond their control, as through widowhood or old age. This neat theoretical symmetry between forms of welfare and types of recipient proved difficult to implement.

The huge amount of Victorian philanthropic resources was divided into endowed and unendowed charities, the products of contemporary and earlier benevolence respectively. In some areas these charitable resources were even greater than those available for distribution under the statutory Poor Law. Endowed charity was frequently in a form – such as almshouses for the old – that made it easy to target it on the deserving. But there were also many small bequests that enjoined the periodic distribution of coals, bread or money that were more difficult to administer discriminatingly. Such 'doles' were even more common in contemporary giving, despite a censorious literature on their 'pauperizing' effects. The principal advocates of a more scientific charity were members of the Charity Organization Society, set up in 1868 to promote the channelling of philanthropy towards the deserving, and thus to prevent a duplication of the efforts of poor-law guardians. This philosophy swiftly influenced the central Poor Law Board which issued the celebrated Goschen Minute of 1869 advocating that guardians should adhere to separate spheres of influence from those of charitable bodies. At the local level co-operation between poor-law guardians and members of the COS continued to be infrequent.[4] And, more generally, it seems doubtful if the advocacy by the COS of 'judicious' rather than 'promiscuous' charity had much lasting impact. In contrast, the methods of social case-work pioneered by the society – in its attempts to investigate applicants' resources and thus to determine their eligibility for aid – proved to be more influential. These Victorian case-workers were predominantly female;[5] an indication of the feminization of charitable work.

Historians have proved to be more cynical than were contemporaries about the nature of Victorian philanthropy; they have pointed both to its controlling functions in relation to its recipients, and to an element of self-interest by its administrators.[6] Women, for example, clearly benefited from their new public role in administering voluntary agencies, since they acquired new skills and enhanced their self-confidence. Recipients of philanthropy found that it was 'aid with strings' since, although charity lacked the stigma of poor relief, it resembled the Poor Law in including an element of social control.

From the patients of voluntary hospitals and dispensaries, through inhabitants of almshouses or pupils in elementary schools run by religious societies, to the inmates of Magdalens, philanthropic institutions attempted to reshape the moral behaviour of those whom they aided, as their rules made clear. Paternalism was thus concerned not only with benevolence but with authority.

During the second half of the nineteenth century many continued to believe that such voluntary endeavour was qualitatively superior to collectivist action, but there was appreciation of its increasing quantitative inadequacy in the face of growing needs. Geographically, philanthropic provision was uneven; its existence was frequently in inverse proportion to the need for it. And the overall resources of voluntary bodies were all too often inadequate to meet the vastly increased demands of a modern industrial society. The case of elementary education is instructive here. The two main religious societies (the National School Society and the British and Foreign School Society) had to be financially aided in their task of providing schools as early as 1833; public grants for such private provision then steadily increased in the mid-nineteenth century; and in 1870 collectivist action was recognized as necessary to 'fill in the gaps' of the voluntary system. This dual system of public and private education – with the latter receiving public funds in return for ceding some autonomy – has continued in modified form to the present day. The extending boundaries of collectivist action did, however, produce much anxiety. The other face of *laissez-faire* was Smilesian self-help, and it was feared that public intervention would weaken individualistic virtues of industry and thrift. Victorian and Edwardian debates on the subject of personal as against public financial provision for old age illustrated the dilemmas clearly. (This topic is in some sense a perennial one, and attracted equally agonized discussion in 1985, with proposals to modify the State Earnings Related Pensions Scheme – SERPS – and alter the balance between state and private pensions.[7]) The issue first surfaced over how poor-law guardians should treat the resources of applicants who were members of friendly societies and who were already receiving some income from their benefits. Central regulations indicated that all income should be taken into account and then deducted from scales of relief so as to achieve uniformity between applicants. But many local guardians recognized that a more important principle was involved than administrative tidiness, and that such action would penalize previous thrift and undercut the impulse of self-help in the labouring class: so they usually compromised by taking into account only part of the benefit. And discussion at the turn of the century over the desirability of a state pension foundered for years on the objection that this would inhibit thrift and the creation of personal savings for future needs.[8]

For much of the twentieth century voluntaryism gave way before the greater vigour of collectivist action. Only as a result of more recent doubts about the ability of the welfare state to deliver optimal services comprehensively has the voluntary principle attracted renewed interest. The concept of a dual system of parallel, and mutually reinforcing, public and private provision had been carried over from the nineteenth to the twentieth century. Both the Majority and Minority Reports on the Poor Law of 1909 envisaged a continuing role for voluntary activity alongside state action, with the Minority Report advocating a partnership in which voluntary bodies extended and supplemented statutory services. In the inter-war period, the squeeze placed on public services by the restrictionist financial policies of central government meant that voluntaryism continued to occupy a strategic position. At this time the vitality of voluntary bodies did not foreshadow their later, more limited role under the classic welfare state. In the high days of the welfare state, in the fifties and sixties, British voluntary bodies were seen – and saw themselves – as a minor supplement of public provision. However, an increasing sensitivity to the range of needs that welfare services were failing to meet meant that from about the late sixties onwards a more favourable view of voluntaryism emerged. Official reports from Seebohm to Wolfenden extolled the desirability of citizen participation in the community, and the virtues of the 'participatory principle' – a new label for an older concept of communal self-help.

Since 1979 the voluntary principle has been seen as even more valuable. The rhetoric of the New Right had denigrated the defects of collectivism and looked forward to 'a better future' when voluntary agencies and family care take on an enhanced role in welfare. Sir Keith Joseph encapsulated the ethos of this movement with the statement that 'inasmuch as personal responsibility has been eroded by a shift of housing, education and welfare provision excessively to the state, we are trying to shift that responsibility'. Recent government proposals to give a more important role to housing associations in the management of public-sector housing, or the expansion of privately run homes for elderly residents (many of whose fees are paid through public benefits), are only the most obvious examples of this shift from public to private. It is also hoped that the economic rewards of individualism in Thatcherite Britain will lead to exercise of social conscience, through an increase in voluntary charitable donations.[9]

A perceptive study by Kramer has argued powerfully, however, that much enthusiasm by both the political right and the left for voluntaryism is naive, and ignores major problems. Amongst these are inadequate resources and unequal geographical coverage (which we have noted were also conspicuous weaknesses of Victorian voluntaryism), as well as lack of accountability, bureaucratic inefficiency, and the inability of private social networks to substitute for statutory services.[10] Apparent enthusiasm for private welfare may be motivated primarily by a desire for budgetary cuts, and may therefore lead to greater difficulties than the collectivist solutions previously castigated as unsatisfactory. The appeal of simplistic policies directed at a mythical golden age remains powerful, however, as can be seen in those presently advocated in the field of informal welfare.

Informal Welfare in the Family and Community

It all really starts in the family, because not only is the family the most important means through which we show our care for others. It's the place where each generation learns its responsibilities towards the rest of society . . . I believe that the volunteer movement is at the heart of all our social welfare provision. That the statutory services are the supportive services underpinning where necessary, filling the gaps, and helping the helpers.[11]

These 'home truths' from the Prime Minister, Margaret Thatcher, were significant in suggesting in 1981 that efforts to roll back the frontiers of the welfare state not only involved a reassertion of the voluntary principle, but also a closely associated revival of private welfare with devolution of increased responsibility to the family. Informal care in the family was viewed as 'natural'. So too was the related care, supplied in informal networks of friends and neighbours, that today is often labelled 'community care'.

Assumptions about a plentiful supply of informal care have tended to be made by public welfare authorities throughout the period covered in this book. To what extent this ideal was ever grounded in reality is difficult to verify, since a fundamental problem in analysing its provision lies in the fact that it is a 'labour of love', and is both a labour and a relationship.[12] Indeed, the re-conceptualization of certain types of unpaid female labour as a welfare service has been a recent achievement of feminist analysis.[13] In practice much care has always been located in the private domain; this female care has been both unpaid and uncounted. Historically, the state has been reluctant to take over, or even to share, responsibility for the main areas of informal care – notably that of very young children, of the physically or mentally handicapped, or of frail, elderly people. In consequence, limited statutory provision has altered the boundary between public and private welfare systems to a much smaller extent than in other areas.[14] A continued reliance on informal care has been based almost entirely on the assumption that there exists a plentiful supply of female labour in the family. In both past and present there has been a strong cultural definition of women as natural carers. This has gone hand in hand with a traditional view of the family as the first line of support for the dependent.

In the Victorian period poor-law authorities were charged with the relief of destitution and in this role gave some support to female carers. But they gave limited help only to restricted categories amongst them; the most fortunate were 'deserving', respectable widows with small children who would usually receive outdoor relief in their own homes; but 'undeserving' cases, such as deserted wives (with similar family circumstances), might be penalized by relief inside the workhouse. Such discrimination arose from concern that familial responsibility was being breached, and that what appeared to be a case of desertion was in reality a wife in collusion with her husband to illegally extract money from public funds.[15] For maintenance purposes poor-law guardians worked with a three-generation definition of the family.[16] As a result, adult children were expected to give care and, where they had sufficient income, often some financial assistance to their aged parents when necessary. Statutory provision for families struggling with the care of physically handicapped members was minimal although in certain large towns a few voluntary institutions existed to give assistance. Some public provision for the care of the severely mentally handicapped existed *de facto* in the lunacy wards of the nineteenth-century workhouse or, to a lesser extent, in the lunatic asylum. This was partly because voluntary 'idiot asylums' were few and far between but, more importantly, because the distinction between mental illness and mental handicap was so little understood that these mentally handicapped people were likely to be certified as mentally ill, and placed in institutions as 'harmless lunatics'. In the twentieth century specialist provision for both mentally and physically handicapped people has improved, but there is still considerable reliance placed on care in the family.

In the early twentieth century little additional material help was given to female carers in the family, despite the development of clinics for mothers and their children. Jane Lewis has argued authoritatively that 'the principal aim of the majority of the child and maternal welfare services was to promote a greater sense of moral responsibility on the part of the mother'.[17] Low-cost educational services were therefore preferred to much-needed help that would have required expenditure – such as family allowances. Inter-war 'welfare feminism', by spearheading the campaign for these allowances and hence for welfare provision for female carers and their dependent children, also reinforced traditionally defined gender roles.[18] The eventual enactment of family allowances in the legislation of the classic welfare state in 1945 owed more to a perceived need to preserve work-incentives than to this feminist pressure. Eleanor Rathbone, the great inter-war campaigner for family allowances, achieved a notable victory by defeating a legislative proposal to pay such allowances to the father rather than the mother.[19] (Forty years later this achievement was almost overturned by a contentious – and eventually unsuccessful – government proposal to pay future child benefits to the father.)

Welfare developments since the forties have provided little overall improvement in statutory support for carers. On the positive side there has been a very limited expansion of public nursery schooling, but this has been almost entirely taken up by the minority of children with 'special needs'. Help for women looking after the frail or disabled at home was in general conspicuous by its absence until 1986, when the European Court ruled that married women were entitled to the Invalid Care Allowance. Previously, this allowance was payable to a relative staying at home to care for a disabled individual, but was *not* payable to a married woman, because she was assumed to be at home in any event. Effectively, as the Equal Opportunities Commission concluded, this excluded 99.5 per cent of those actually giving care. And the 'invisibility' of these carers leads to a continued disregard of their needs. [20]

Insidious changes in the ideal of community care have placed additional pressure on the female carer at home. This has cut across a legislative commitment to equality between the sexes. [21] In the fifties and sixties the drive for community care meant replacing care in isolated institutions (often a legacy from the Poor Law), with that in buildings located *in* the community. By the seventies the concept was also implying care *by* the community. And by the eighties care in the community was increasingly seen as being *instead* of expensive involvement by the social services. [22] With an ageing population, and decreasing institutional provision for the old relative to their numbers, increased reliance on home care for the elderly seems inescapable. But cutbacks in the support services of home helps etc. – which even at their present level are already inadequate to meet current needs – make it even clearer that community care is seen by the government as a cost-cutting device. Titmuss's earlier warning about community care was prophetic: 'what some hope one day will exist is suddenly thought by many to exist already'. [23]

Fiscal and Occupational Welfare

Fiscal and occupational welfare – like the voluntary sector and informal care – has only relatively recently attracted much discussion. Titmuss drew attention to the existence of 'differential development' in welfare, and suggested the inadequacy of assumptions that labelled one set of state interventions as social services within 'the welfare state', while leaving out of the analysis a much broader area of intervention with similar objectives. He argued that although tax allowances in 'fiscal welfare' were accounting conveniences rather than the cash transactions in social service expenditure, the ensuing tax saving to the individual was 'in effect a transfer payment'.[24] Others have denied this by suggesting that a reduction in tax cannot be treated as a form of welfare payment, since there is no unrequited grant to the recipient, but merely a reduction in the tax that would otherwise be collected. In my view, an appropriate response to this line of reasoning is to suggest that the focus for analysis is not the form of accounting but of service. And I find it a convincing rationale for seeing as part of fiscal welfare such items as tax relief on life assurance premiums and mortgage relief granted to owner-occupiers, that these lend support to services that the state might otherwise have to provide in the form, for example, of widows' pensions or council housing. Mortgage relief is therefore to be seen as analogous to a rent subsidy to council-house tenants. This would not be an uncontentious position since some would deny that the two are comparable; even a government housing policy review dismissed the possibility of comparison in 1977, because it would be like comparing 'chalk and cheese'.[25] The third area of differentiated welfare isolated by Titmuss was occupational welfare – benefits in cash and kind by employers, but ultimately receiving a substantial subsidy from the Exchequer.[26] Some components – such as occupational pensions and subsidized health insurance – clearly supply private alternatives to state-provided welfare and for this reason are discussed in this chapter. Other components in the form of fringe benefits (such as company cars and subsidized meals), which have been discussed elsewhere as a private market welfare state,[27] have a less obvious claim to be regarded as welfare rather than remuneration, and I have therefore excluded them. The subject of fiscal and occupational welfare thus remains both contentious and complex.[28]

The state's support through tax relief for private provision of pensions, housing, health and education had its origin in the Victorian period. Over the years the amount of such support has grown considerably. Its enhanced value is partly the result of a more extensive system of income tax. In Victorian days only the affluent paid tax whereas today the tax threshold on incomes comes much lower. Also, the growth of a progressive system of income tax since

1909, with higher taxes on unearned income and on larger incomes, has made such tax privileges much more valuable to the individual taxpayer. The introduction of capital gains tax in 1965 enhanced the attractiveness of certain forms of saving – house-ownership or life assurance, for example – since the proceeds are exempt from capital gains tax. By 1983/4 such tax subsidies have been calculated as worth £5,435 million for owner-occupation (mortgage interest relief, capital gains tax exemption, and stamp duty exemption), and £820 million for life assurance (income tax exemption on premiums and capital gains tax exemption on proceeds), while that for pensions amounted to £1,760 million.[29] These constituted the most important elements in fiscal welfare. Given the amounts lost it is predictable that the Treasury should periodically impose restrictions on such tax privileges. Life assurance schemes during the First World War, lump sum payments in 'top hat' schemes after the Second World War or, more recently, mortgage interest relief on second homes, and new assurance premiums, have all attracted the attention of Chancellors of the Exchequer. In part this has been because of their revenue-hungry nature and, in part, because such substantial tax reliefs are an impediment to a radical reform of the tax structure that would give a lower general rate of tax and expand the area of individual choice.

Let us now examine in more detail the growth of fiscal and occupational welfare. We look first at the subject of provision for old age; the extent to which private pensions and related life assurance policies are assisted by the Exchequer. Traditionally, the state has seen it as desirable for the individual to make provision for future needs and has encouraged this through tax incentives. In 1853 Gladstone had first given tax relief to life assurance premiums, and this concession lasted until 1984. Already, by the end of the nineteenth century, about one in five taxpayers had availed themselves of it. In earlier days such concessions benefited the very small minority with large incomes who alone paid tax but, from the 1940s onwards, the extension of income tax to a much larger proportion of the population was one factor increasing the appeal of these benefits. Earlier, in 1921, an even better deal had been given to certain approved pension schemes, under which their funds gained tax exemption. During and after the Second World War very high rates of taxation on companies meant that with this tax relief, pensions could be provided at virtually zero cost. And, since all except the lowest income earners now paid income tax, there was an equivalent appeal to larger numbers of employees to save for their old age in this tax-efficient way. By the seventies these substantial tax incentives taken together had stimulated about a third of personal savings in Britain to be in the form of pensions, a much higher proportion than in other countries. The evolving forms of tax concession also influenced the way in which pensions came to be paid, as in the spectacular growth in lump sum provision during the seventies, from one-third to nine-tenths of all such schemes.

The proportion of the workforce covered by private occupational pension schemes has grown very considerably as a result not only of their tax advantages but also because of demographic and employment changes in the numbers that can expect to enjoy a period of retirement. Whereas in 1900 only 0.1 million occupational pensions were paid, by 1979 there were 3.7 million recipients.[30] And a reduction of the relative role to be played by SERPS in relation to that by private provision is likely to increase this number still further. Preserved rights in pension schemes make it difficult to modify the pension system as it has evolved over the years, despite attacks by both radical right and left. Defence of existing tax privileges on pensions is as widespread as its beneficiaries, and ranges from the City to the membership of trade unions.

Even more broad-based in its self-interested support is the subsidy given to owner-occupiers through tax relief on mortgage interest payments. While the sum eligible for such relief has been limited (in 1987 it is £30,000), it is worth more to high income groups who pay tax at the highest rates. But despite widespread agreement that it is socially inequitable, drives up house prices and distorts the provision of different types of housing, action to end it is seen as politically very dangerous by all parties. Limitation of the relief to the standard rate is the most radical action contemplated at present. We have seen that mortgage interest relief, together with tax exemption on the capital gains made from the sale of an owner-occupied house, forms the largest component in the fiscal welfare state. And, since two-thirds of homes were in owner-occupation by 1987, there is a uniquely powerful interest group defending the status quo.

Private health insurance has been boosted recently by its inclusion within occupational welfare. In the inter-war years, before the advent of the National Health Service, private health insurance was taken out quite widely by individual members of the middle classes, who were excluded from free treatment in voluntary hospitals or by panel doctors. During the first decades of the NHS the perceived need for private insurance was much diminished and there was only a modest growth in subscribers to these private schemes from the fifties to the early seventies. But the decision of the Labour government to tax health insurance premiums, and their intention to phase out private paybeds from NHS hospitals, then contributed to a sharp decline in private subscribers. Between 1974 and 1977 those covered by private health insurance fell from 2.3 to 1 million. However, individual subscriptions again became more buoyant after the 1979 election brought a different set of expectations about private and state health services. Even more significant was the growth in occupational insurance schemes; in the eighties health insurance became the fourth most popular fringe benefit – after life assurance, company cars and subsidized food. The proportion of individual subscriptions to private health insurance companies fell, but those paid by employers under company purchase schemes rose, as did employee purchase schemes, whereby a firm or trade union negotiated a group discount subscription that was then paid by individual members. The state encouraged the extension of company purchase schemes to blue-collar workers and, in 1981, tax relief was allowed for this purpose for workers earning less than £8,500 annually. Three years later, companies were allowed to set against corporation tax the health insurance premiums they paid for all employees. This concession was estimated to be worth £30 million annually. This contributed to a growth in the numbers with private health insurance from an estimated 2.7 million people in 1979 to 5.7 million in 1987.[31]

As with private education, the contribution made by the general taxpayer to private welfare is not confined to tax privileges given to the individual, but is also given to associated institutions – hospitals or schools. From its inception the National Health Service has contained a private component; its hospitals have had from 1 to 2 per cent of paybeds, and part-time hospital consultants have had the right to undertake private practice. While the availability and use of paybeds has been declining since the mid-seventies, the liberalization of consultants' contracts in 1980 (enabling full-timers to do private work) has resulted in a notable increase in the amount of private practice undertaken by them. This has materially helped in a notable expansion of private hospitals; between 1979 and 1985 there has been an increase of one-third in their numbers, and a growth of one-half in the number of private acute beds within them. But the full extent to which the NHS effectively subsidizes the private sector – as, for example, through the supply of staff trained at public expense, or the use of NHS pathology and radiology services – has so far generated more ideological heat than evidential light.

By the early eighties, one in thirteen people were covered by private health insurance; a larger proportion than the one in seventeen pupils who attended public (i.e. private) schools.[32] The cost of the latter's education was subsidized by the general taxpayer in varied ways. For instance, their school fees may avoid capital transfer tax if parents invest a capital sum through an annuity trust scheme, or if grandparents invest in an education trust. Private schools also benefit considerably from the advantages accruing to them from their charitable status; this exempts them from income, capital gains and corporation taxes, and also gives them rate relief. In addition, these schools may have the advantage of staff who have been educated or trained at the state's expense. And there is a further input of public money through the considerable number of pupils at private schools paid for by public bodies: children of parents in the diplomatic corps or in the armed services are eligible for boarding allowances, and local education authorities may buy places at independent schools. In addition, an Assisted Places scheme was started by the Conservative government in 1981, whereby private schools could offer a limited number of places for pupils from the state sector, which were then paid for with public money.

Fiscal and occupational welfare is of much greater extent than is generally perceived, and its growth has accelerated since 1979. This type of welfare is not now exclusively the province of the wealthiest members of society, although it is heavily concentrated among the more affluent. The impact of more widely diffused pension rights or of house ownership has been to extend the ownership of wealth. But, as with the provisions of the classic welfare state, its incremental growth has produced anomalies and social inequities. This has meant that it has been attacked by both the radical left and the radical right. For the latter, the large sums tied up in piecemeal fashion in fiscal and occupational welfare prevent a more logical tax structure in which lower tax rates would permit unfettered individual choice in welfare. And the former argues that fiscal and occupational welfare is a public subsidy to the better-off; it compounds the deficiencies of the classic welfare state in this respect.

The complexities of the interaction between overlapping states of welfare – whether described in the convenient shorthand of private and public, or of formal and informal, welfare – are attracting an increased amount of attention. There is a better appreciation of the large extent to which fiscal and occupational welfare, as well as much state provision, benefits the affluent more than the poor.[33] (Just how much they do so is problematical since calculations typically fail to make explicit the counterfactual assumptions being used.) The limited egalitarian impact of welfare provision has led some to question the value of this indirect method, and to propose the adoption of a more direct assault on income inequality. Similarly, feminists have drawn attention to the social injustices that welfare policies imply for women; the proposed retreat from formal, collectivist provision is predicated on the assumption of women's informal care for the young, the sick, the disabled and the elderly in the family. Current assumptions about women's role in society appear as patriarchal when extended to private welfare, as they have done in the past, when the values informing public welfare have produced gender discrimination in benefits.[34] Contemporary attitudes towards the welfare state, and expectations of its future role in society, are discussed more fully in the next chapter.

VII

Views from the Eighties

The shift to a more restrictionist model of welfare under the Thatcher ministries has too often been discussed in Britain as if it were a purely national phenomenon. While it is evident that many of the values and assumptions that *shape* it are derived from British tradition, our earlier discussion has indicated that it is part of an international *response* to a perceived crisis in welfare. It also partakes of a general shift to the political right. The influence on British practice of social policies initiated by neo-liberals in the USA has become increasingly plain, not least because reforming initiatives are often accompanied by ministerial fact-finding visits across the Atlantic.[1] At a more general level the influence of an enterprise culture – practised most forcefully in the USA – has probably been even greater. A prominent Conservative concluded in 1988, 'I believe that modern conservatism has done more to create fairness by spreading wealth than the socialism of 1945 did by what was in effect spreading poverty.'[2] In this interpretation it is only in Thatcherite Britain that Oliver Twist would get a second helping from the surplus created by an enterprise society.

It is customary to see a welfare divide as occurring after 1979; Thatcherism is viewed by both the political right and the left as having broken with a bi-partisan consensus that had lasted from the forties to the late seventies. Writing in 1980, Brian Abel-Smith judged that until that point there had been a consensus on maintaining the main fabric of the welfare state, so that political debate had arisen only over how much to spend on further developments.[3] Yet closer scrutiny reveals some problems with this interpretation. A fundamental reason for this is that the basis of that agreement was the Beveridge Report, an ambiguous and eclectic document that was less bedrock than shifting sand. As José Harris has perceptively noted, Beveridge provided 'a portmanteau set of ideas offering all things to all men', so that 'people could find in Beveridge whatever they chose'.[4] In the immediate post-Beveridge years a mood of social cohesiveness – reinforced by common experience of wartime and post-war austerities – fostered universalist welfare policies; for once the welfare state was supported by the values of a welfare society. This distinctive society soon disappeared. Even Beveridge had concluded by 1953 that 'the picture of yesterday's hopeful collaboration in curing evils of want and disease and squalor . . . looks like a dream today'.[5]

By this time Labour, the party identified with the classic welfare state, had been replaced in government by the Conservative party, whose attitude to Beveridge's recommendations had been ambivalent at the time. While official party policy in the early fifties was to continue with the welfare state (the 'Butskellite' consensus), some members of the party advocated minimalist welfare provision: 'We believe that it [i.e. the state] should provide a minimum standard, above which people should be free to rise as far as their industry, thrift, their ability or genius may take them.'[6] This statement by the One Nation Group (whose authors included the later Prime Minister Edward Heath) appears significant in historical perspective. It was consistent with the more individualistic statements in the Beveridge Report, yet foreshadowed later policy developments that undercut some of the report's central recommendations. And a pamphlet on the social services, published by the Conservative Political Centre in 1952, went even further than the Thatcherite revolution has yet done, in stating that 'the question . . . is not "should a means test be applied to a social service?" but "why should any social service be provided *without* a test of need?"'[7]

Did this opening of the debate between universalists and selectivists break the consensus over welfare, or was it so much hot air floating over continuing bi-partisan practice? Resolving this central issue depends crucially on our interpretation – collectivist or individualistic – of the Beveridge Report, and on our perception of what comprises the main fabric of the welfare state. If we define the latter in conventional terms – as the provision by the state through insurance and/or taxation of adequate income and basic social services to meet the main contingencies in life – then one might conclude that a broad consensus was maintained through the fifties and sixties in social security provision and in health, and this applied also in the maintenance of a policy of full employment. Yet already there were partisan differences in education and housing since the Labour party pursued more socially egalitarian and interventionist policies (in the priority given to council housing, rent control, and a vigorous promotion of comprehensive schooling), while the Conservatives gave greater prominence to market mechanisms and the freedom of the individual to benefit from a more affluent society (in the de-control of rents, the promotion of private house-building, and the support given to tripartite education with a continuance of grammar schools). Viewed from the contemporary perspective of the sixties, differences in social ethos and in policy made it then appear that the welfare consensus had been dissipated and a 'battle-ground' had ensued.[8] With the passage of years it is clear that a limited consensus had continued on a central area of welfare, but that beyond this partisan values emphasized either individualistic or universalistic elements within the Beveridgean framework. Under the Conservative administration of Heath from 1970–4 a notable growth in means-tested benefits served notice of a practical adherence to the selectivism and more minimalist social welfare that had been advocated theoretically twenty years before. By the early seventies, with the ending of the commitment of full employment policies and renewed concern for the work-incentives and educational standards, Economic Man began again to assume a higher profile than Welfare Man. The worsening problems of the economy made universality in welfare increasingly Utopian even to Labour, so that – despite a widening of the ideological gap on welfare between the parties during the seventies – the policies of the later Labour government under Callaghan displayed some continuity with those of Heath.

A review of the course of the bi-partisan agreement on welfare indicates that a long-term erosion had occurred. Yet, despite this evidence that the Butskellite consensus involved a substantial measure of partisan disagreement, it is obvious that the same rule book (Beveridge) was deployed by each side. Beyond these fraternal struggles within the Beveridgean welfare microcosm, more fundamental questions were being posed. In their potential for controversy these placed into perspective the relatively small magnitude of post-war political contention over social policy. The future direction of welfare was once more being debated within traditional polarities of a wider *laissez-faire* or collectivist macrocosm, as had been usual in the Victorian and Edwardian eras. From the late fifties the Institute of Economic Affairs took up the torch of an anti-collectivist tradition that ran from Adam Smith to Hayek. It extolled the efficiency, as well as the economic and political neutrality, of the market in providing choices in welfare. In the seventies the Centre for Policy Studies was set up to provide more radical views than the orthodoxies of the Conservative Research Department at that time. And the Adam Smith Institute, on the basis of public choice theory, concerned itself with practical and incremental policy proposals that would lead away from welfare-statism. The beneficiary of these 'think tanks' was Margaret Thatcher. She was the first openly to challenge the Butskellite consensus and to acknowledge that her government's policies no longer adhered to it.

Ideologically the break had occurred, yet practically there was substantial continuity in the first two Thatcher governments with what had gone before. The economic implications of recession had earlier made the Callaghan government admit that 'the party's over'. It had begun to cut housing and education expenditure, and it was in these same areas that the succeeding Conservative administration had its successes in containing welfare expenditure. But the first Thatcher government's economic policies – in intensifying unemployment – made the fulfilment of its restrictionist social policies impossible to attain in the short run, since the social security bill became higher rather than lower. Figure 1 (p. 73) shows the rapidly rising expenditure on social security as a percentage of GDP in the United Kingdom at this time. Figure 2 (p. 105) indicates the breakdown of expenditure on social security and shows the increasing proportion taken up by unemployment benefit and, even more, by the rapid growth in supplementary benefit, on which the long-term unemployed are dependent. Figure 2 also shows the long-term importance of state spending on retirement pensions. Despite pensions' declining share in social security expenditure the actual sums involved have shown very substantial growth. Between 1979 and

1985 the cost of UK pensions increased very rapidly from £8,563 to £16,161 million. Rhetoric rather than the reality of welfare reform thus had largely to bridge the gap between 1979 and the beginning of radical change in 1987/8. The early eighties may, therefore, be seen as an ironic counterpoint to the years from the fifties to the seventies; the earlier years of consensus hid substantial disagreement and discontinuity, whereas the end of consensus concealed a measure of accord and continuity.

Welfare and the Economy

Full appreciation that the classic welfare state was a 'residual beneficiary of the Growth State'[9] came with the stagflation of the mid- and late seventies. For some this economic downturn discredited post-war Keynesian economic management. Bacon and Eltis's interpretation provided an alternative pointer to future government policy in suggesting that the British economy was performing so badly because an 'unproductive' public sector soaked up labour which could otherwise be put to more productive use in the private sector.[10] Excessive state spending on welfare was thus seen as constituting one basic cause of poor British economic performance. The tenets of Milton Friedman and the Chicago School became influential on the political right: the market rather than the political process was the efficient way to make decisions. That greater freedom and individual well-being would follow from a diminution of government activity was the inference that would later be drawn from these and kindred analyses by the New Right in Thatcherite Britain and Reaganite America.

A speech in 1974 by Sir Keith Joseph signalled the kind of shift in thinking that was occurring in the Thatcherite wing of the Conservative party:

First, for the past thirty years in our party-competitive efforts to improve life, we have overburdened the economy. We have over-estimated the power of government to do more and more for more and more people, to re-shape the economy, and indeed human society, according to blueprints. We have tried to take short cuts to Utopia . . . we have finished up further away than ever. In the social services, alas, we seem to have generated more

Figure 2: UK Social Security Expenditure in 1951, 1971 and 1985

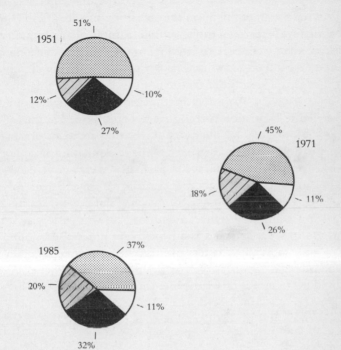

 Retirement Pensions

 Unemployment Benefit and Supplementary Benefits

Other Benefits, including Family Allowances, and Invalidity, Disablement, Sickness, Maternity, Death, and Industrial Injury Benefits

Other Expenditure including Local Welfare Services, and Goods and Services, including Administration

Source: National Income and Expenditure (Central Statistical Office)

problems than we have solved . . . Secondly, for thirty years, levels of state expenditure have been greater than the economy could bear. The private sector, the productive sector has been weighed down by the burden of taxation.[11]

The reference to problems in the social services was far-sighted; the disfunctional aspects of the growth in complexity and rigidity in the welfare state were later to become much more visible. The power held by the public-sector unions during the 'winter of discontent' of 1978–9 was a significant factor both in the electoral failure of the Labour party in 1979 and in the growth of public support for Thatcherite legislation curbing trade union power in the following years. Work-floor productivity in relation to work practices was seen by the New Right as in need of the re-animating discipline of the market. Public-sector unions in particular were perceived as constituting an impediment to the creation of an efficient market in welfare. The market possessed not only static but dynamic advantages in leading to growth and a more affluent society. Capitalism was in this sense depicted as a benevolent process; economic initiative and individual enterprise would improve overall living standards. The poor (as well as the rich) would benefit, since they would be members of a wealthier (but more unequal) society.

This theme of the interdependence of economic and social policy has been central to the Thatcherite perception of the changes that have occurred since 1979. 'We now have a new Britain, confident, optimistic, sure of its economic strength,' rejoiced the Prime Minister in her address to the Conservative Conference after her third successive electoral victory in 1987.[12] Her pride was rooted in the recent successes of the British economy after the difficult years of 'financial discipline' from 1979 to 1983. From the standpoint of the political right, private enterprise had been stimulated by the government's squeeze on public spending; from a peak of 46.5 per cent in 1982 it had fallen to 43.3 per cent of GDP by 1986, and is projected to fall even further. Equally important in these perceptions were cuts in tax rates. Since 1979, the investment surcharge had been abolished, the basic rate had fallen from 33 to 25 per cent and top rates had been reduced even further from 98 to 40 per cent – the lowest in Europe. By 1988 the economy was in its seventh year of economic growth and real GDP was a fifth higher than it had been in 1979.[13] A combination of sound money, weaker trade unions, the superior efficiency of private over public concerns, and the stimulus given to individual enterprise was officially given most of the credit.

Economically and socially the effect of these changes was to make the divide between the Two Nations of the employed and the unemployed – the wage-earner and the welfare-dependent – much starker. During these years the majority of the population gained economically; average real disposable household income rose at 2.5 per cent per year. After the first four years (when two million jobs had been lost), employment slowly rose – with the addition of half a million jobs by 1986. Property-owning became more widespread; by 1988 three-fifths of the population owned or were buying their housing, and one-fifth owned shares.[14] But contrasting with these indicators of an affluent property-owning democracy were other signs that showed that the gap between rich and poor had widened. Homelessness increased; the number of those in temporary bed-and-breakfast accommodation trebled between 1983 and 1986. Income inequality grew in the first four Thatcher years, reversing a fifty-year trend towards greater equality. By 1983 the post tax income of the top 10 per cent of income earners had come to exceed the cumulative total of the bottom 50 per cent. Poverty had also risen, with nearly one in three living on or just above the official poverty line; the numbers had increased from 11.5 million in 1979 to 16.3 million in 1983. The health gap between rich and poor also grew sharply in the same period, as could be seen through a comparison of the morbidity and mortality rates of unskilled male workers with those of professional and managerial men.[15]

These socio-economic changes of the eighties were seen by the New Right as an extension to the people of opportunity and choice. Seizing a populist position more recently occupied by the left, Thatcher has claimed 'an irreversible shift of power in favour of working people and their families'.[16] By taking the high ground of social policy, the radical initiatives of the Tory governments have been remarkably successful in placing opposition parties in a merely reactive position. Labour, as the largest parliamentary opposition party, relied on a comprehensive defence of the classic welfare state, and overlooked such unpopular features as its unresponsive housing bureaucracies or self-interestedly powerful public-sector unions. The Alliance (now the Social and Liberal Democrats) has promoted more forward-looking policies, but in turn has forgotten the disadvantages of innovative over-complexity. With a divided opposition, the right's message of the freedom given by material prosperity has been invincible in electoral terms.

In the first two Tory ministries the economic groundwork was laid for the radical social initiatives of the third, although a foretaste of the latter was given in 1980 with the start of council-house sales. The opening years were notable mainly for the short sharp shock of 'sound money' expressed in high interest rates and a strong pound (which contributed to rapidly escalating unemployment levels), and for the beginning of a sustained onslaught on trade union powers. During the second term, which began in 1983, privatization (or de-nationalization) assumed great symbolical importance. Its rationale was seen at first as increasing efficiency or raising revenue, but its longer-term political significance seems likely to be in strengthening the market through eliminating public-sector jobs. In social terms its effect in introducing popular capitalism, through increasing the ownership of shares, has perhaps been exaggerated. It has led on in the third Thatcherite term of office to an ambitious social pro-gramme; this is promoted as an extention of opportunity and freedom of choice to the people in education, housing and health. Margaret Thatcher has interpreted it as an ongoing revolutionary process, 'a staging post on a much longer journey'.[17]

The nature of this planned social revolution owes much more to the character and opinions of the Prime Minister, Margaret Thatcher, than historically has been the case in earlier periods of radical change. Strong convictions, an intolerance of opposition, and great physical energy have contributed to her political domi-nance of the Conservative party and cabinet. Guided by political instinct rather than prolonged reflection she is a believer in the political imperative of action, and of confrontation rather than conciliation. Freed from the constraints of national economic weak-ness to an extent unequalled by her post-war predecessors, and unhampered by effective parliamentary opposition, the third Thatcher government has the power to make decisive social reforms equivalent in their scope to earlier periods of radical change – as in the 'Victorian welfare state' of the 1830s and 1840s, the creation of the Edwardian 'social service' state in the 1900s, or the 'classic welfare state' of the 1940s. The character of these reforms will bear an indelible Thatcherite imprint; an autocratic populism that justifies a notable increase in the power of central government by the need for strong action to free the people from bondage to their local councils. Reforms in council housing, local authority schools, and the rating system aim to 'greatly reduce the power of the local council over tenants, parents and business'. And a distinctive blend of moralistic materialism, drawing on 'the moral energy of society'[18] – while appealing strongly to economic self-interest, which is thereby made respectable – seems likely to revive the ethos of the Victorian age of self-help.

The extent of the shift to 'a different vision' of welfare from that in the classic welfare state was made clear in a keynote speech in 1987 by the Secretary of State for the Social Services, John Moore. This was given shortly after his return from a visit to the United States of America where he had studied libertarian views of welfare and looked at workfare. He stated that '1987 is very different from 1947 . . . Life has changed, people's expectations have changed and it's necessary for what we call our welfare state to change as well.' Significantly, the basic requirement of social policy into the twenty-first century was seen as moving welfare recipients 'away from dependency and towards opportunity'. In his view,

A welfare state worthy of the name aims at the real welfare of its citizens. It works to widen the understanding that dependency can be debilitating and that the best kind of help is that which gives people the will and ability to help themselves.[19]

This signalled a prospective move into a minimalist welfare world that was both a reaction to the recent past and a revival of a more distant one.

In the immediate future it seems probable that the state will move to being much more of an enabler, and less of a provider, with a correspondingly enhanced role given to the voluntary sector in welfare. Certain kinds of welfare assistance – supplementary benefits or income supplements – may no longer be 'indiscriminate' but, where possible, will be made conditional. These may include work tests (as in American-style workfare, where benefits are payable in return for work), or means tests (that are self-targeting and require a self-definition of poverty). The latter may be perceived (both by recipients and the public) as involving second-class citizenship. This stick-and-carrot approach to welfare dependency is in certain respects reminiscent of the self-acting workhouse test of the nineteenth century.[20] It also strikingly resembles the bifurcated welfare system that has been created in the USA since the New Deal, where there has been a sharp distinction in government provision for – and public perceptions of – social security provision such as pensions, and assistance programmes. Only the latter are stigmatized as 'welfare'.[21] British policies coupling incentives for Victorian-style self-help and opportunity with an attack on certain kinds of welfare dependency seem likely to result eventually in a residual and increasingly marginalized group of poor people.

The combined effect of the Budget of March 1988 with the restructuring of welfare benefits in the Social Security Act of the following month has deepened the divide between rich and poor. The redistributive thrust of Thatcherite policies was illustrated particularly clearly in the contrast between these budgetary hand-outs to the rich and welfare cuts to the poor. Under the former, the top 1 per cent of taxpayers received more from tax cuts than did the bottom 70 per cent. Those earning below the European Commission's 'decency threshold' of £135 per week benefited minimally from the Budget, while for the three million who paid no tax there was no advantage. Progressive taxation as a tool for equality (in which the rich had provided help for the poor), which had been axiomatic since Lloyd George's People's Budget of 1909, was rejected. This strikingly regressive 1988 Budget was seen by Thatcher as 'an epitaph for socialism'.[22] Effectively this meant that under Thatcherite ideology, a low-tax, market economy would give prosperity for the majority, while a minority of the low-waged, the unemployed, and those dependent on welfare would constitute 'an underclass'. Government's role in relation to social justice had been redefined; rather than attempting to narrow the gap between the rich and the very poor, as had been the case since 1945, it was widened.

Radical Policies

'There's a lot to be done to change the dependency-creating aspects of the social security arrangements,' commented that guru of modern Conservatism, Lord Joseph of Portsoken.[23] Yet the scope for such initiatives appears more limited in practice than such rhetoric might suggest. Despite attempts to cut back on social security expenditure through incremental reductions in the real value of certain benefits, expenditure in real terms increased by 43 per cent between 1979 and the end of 1987, when it cost £44 billion.[24] Increased numbers of the elderly, the long-term sick and disabled, single-parent families and the unemployed, accounted for much of this growth. And government spending plans acknowledged that even more money would have to be spent in 1988–90 because of an assumed further increase in numbers of lone parents, and sick and disabled people, as well as to give income support for those faced with increased payments resulting from rate reform. Faced with these constraints was there scope for forcing decisive changes in the dependency culture?

The Social Security Act, that came into effect in April 1988, is intended to 'target help on those who most need it and to control the growth of public expenditure', according to the Secretary of State for the Social Services.[25] Whether the number that will be advantaged by these structural changes outnumber those who will be disadvantaged is hotly disputed. But particular provisions suggest that targeting help can be welfare-speak for focusing cuts on the poorest and most vulnerable members of our society. A Social Fund will replace the preceding system of single payments for items of special need – bedding, furniture, or clothing – by a much smaller cash-limited provision consisting predominantly of loans.[26] The cash limits imply that there will be redistribution *between* the poorest groups in society, since claimants will be competing amongst themselves for a finite amount of money. Impoverished claimants from the fund also seem likely to face increased indebtedness, with automatic reductions in benefit of from 10 to 15 per cent to repay loans for essential items of household expenditure. Other legislative changes will chip away at the sea-wall of protection that benefits give against poverty, rather than unleash a tide of radical reform to sweep away the 'culture of dependency'. Under the Income Support Scheme, all recipients will have to pay part of their rates for the first time, and benefits for those aged under 25 will also be cut. Housing benefit will be aligned with income support so that many fewer people will in future be eligible, and so that the taper rates (under which benefits will be withdrawn as income rises) will become steeper. Child benefit – condemned as 'ill-targeted' by Moore because of its universality[27] – has been frozen in cash terms and its real value has therefore been eroded. But the intention is that three million children in poorer families will be better off because of additional resources targeted in a new system of Family Credits that replaces Family Income Supplement. Future pensions under SERPS (the State Earnings Related Pension Scheme) have been modified so that benefits will be reduced and the eventual long-term cost to government will halve. The importance of this reform is indicated by Figure 2 (p. 105), which indicates that retirement pensions form the largest element in social security spending. Overall, in its attempt to make a more coherent scheme, the Act has predictably introduced new inequities – most notably between new and old claimants. Those who appear most likely to lose from these multiple changes in social security are a diverse group consisting of pensioners and young unemployed adults, together with some sick and disabled people.

Attempts in the late eighties to slim down social security face the same kind of problems encountered 150 years earlier by the minimalist New Poor Law. In practice, welfare dependency is principally concentrated among the 'helpless poor' not among the 'able-bodied' or 'feckless' poor (well able to earn a living if they are forced to do so), on which reductionist rhetoric had focused. Reforming objectives must therefore be salvaged by policies aimed at the much smaller number of claimants who might potentially be able to participate in the labour market. In the mid-eighties this has meant the construction of increasingly elaborate training and employment schemes.

The new Employment Service (set up in October 1987) will attempt to make these more cohesive and effective by combining responsibility for job schemes *and* for dole provision. Government

concern over the genuine availability of the unemployed for work
will also lead to a drive to make sure that social security is not being
abused. The White Paper on Employment of February 1988 estimated that in one in five cases there were 'serious doubts' about this.[28]
To combat this there will be, on the one hand, a larger team of fraud
investigators and, on the other, greater efforts to get the longer-term
unemployed off benefits and back into work. For example, under the
Restart Programme of 1986 – which concerned itself with those out
of work for more than six months – the jobless have been called for
interview at local Job Centres with the stated objective of getting
them into a training scheme or back into the labour market. Restart
operated not only with a carrot but a stick; if the unemployed
declined an interview three times, they were told they could lose
their benefit. And under the terms of the Employment Bill, every
unemployed person will be invited to a Restart interview every six
months, for as long as they remain unemployed. The conditionality
of benefit on willingness to work seems likely to assume even greater
importance in the future. In an experimental scheme in south-east
London, warnings will be given to long-term unemployed people
that benefit may be jeopardized if they refuse to accept jobs after
visiting Job Clubs.[29] (Interestingly in this context, these Job Clubs
were themselves an import from the USA of a component in new-
style 'voluntary' workfare.) Increased penalties for voluntarily leaving the labour market have also been introduced recently in Britain
in the form of cancelled or diminished benefits. The chairman of the
government's Social Security Advisory Committee, Peter Barclay,
referred to this as 'the English version of Workfare'.[30]

A number of the government's training and employment policies
either contain a workfare component or the potential for its inclusion. Workfare is usually interpreted to mean that those who refuse
to participate in training or employment lose state benefits. It is
important to appreciate both the variety of workfare schemes and
the different social philosophies that may underpin them. For
example, two countries with very different attitudes and provision
for social welfare – the USA and Sweden – both operate workfare
schemes. The American states that operate either voluntary or
compulsory workfare often justify them by reference to the work
ethic; the assumption that those who are on benefits have a duty to

work, and may contribute to society for their welfare through work. In contrast, in Swedish workfare there is a greater emphasis on integrating the individual into society through the labour market by means of high-quality training schemes. In both Swedish and American schemes the cost of each training place is far higher than that envisaged in this country.[31] In Britain workfare is largely perceived in pejorative terms; the right dislikes the expense involved in setting up training schemes, while the left sees any element of compulsion as anathema. Ministers therefore feel the need to deny that workfare is in fact on the agenda. Before the 1987 election the Employment Minister stated that the government 'has no plans to introduce a workfare type programme in this country'. During the debates on the Employment Bill, the present Minister stated that the reforms 'will not lead remorselessly to compulsion', and hence to workfare.[32] Nevertheless, it is becoming clear that this is what a number of initiatives, linking benefit and employment, have the potential to become. From the left it has been pointed out that Clause 26 of the Employment Act designates the Employment Training Scheme as an approved scheme, which then permits benefit to be conditional on acceptance of a training place. Suspicions remain that the bill comprises creeping compulsion.[33] And from the right, the *Economist* has suggested that the proposals signal 'Forward to the Workfare State'.[34]

Employment schemes have increasingly focused on two overlapping groups: the long-term unemployed and the out-of-work young adult. Taking employment and training schemes together with restrictive changes in social security, housing benefit, and the ending of the protection of young people's wages through official Wages Councils, it is clear that the government has targeted the young adult in policies that are designed to replace 'welfare dependency' by the rigours and hardships of the economic market. The rationale for this effort has been clearly put by the Social Services Secretary:

Is it right to draw young people into a benefit culture when the opportunity is there for the taking to acquire the skills and experience to get on to the employment ladder, to be independent and self-reliant?[35]

The main subjects of workfare in Britain have been sixteen and seventeen years olds through the Youth Training Scheme (YTS).

YTS began in 1983 and has been extended from one to two years for participants. It is an ambitious scheme that guarantees to the unemployed school-leaver both training and work experience. The scheme is depicted officially as 'a universal opportunity',[36] but choice will be effectively removed from the individual. Under the provisions of the forthcoming Social Security and Employment Bills a general entitlement to benefit by sixteen and seventeen year olds is removed. Those who are in this age-range but who are not in work, or who turn down a place on YTS, will be denied benefit, unless they can prove 'severe hardship'.

For the long-term unemployed aged from eighteen to twenty-four a guaranteed place, combining work and training, will be found in the Employment Training Scheme (ETS). In 1988 this will replace five existing schemes, including the ill-fated Job Training Scheme (JTS)[37] and the much-criticized Community Programme.[38] The new programme aims to give access to work provided by a company, charity or council. A bonus on top of benefit will be paid, as well as expenses for travel, lodging and childcare. The objective is to provide 600,000 training places annually with an average of six months' training but with the option for participants to continue for up to twelve months.

How successful have the government's employment and training schemes been in reducing unemployment? At the beginning of 1988 there were 2.6 million registered unemployed: of these 1.5 million had been out of work for six months or more, and nearly 0.5 million had not had work for two or more years.[39] Under Restart nearly one in three of those interviewed were recommended either to training schemes run by the Manpower Services Commission (mainly to JTS) or were encouraged to start independent businesses under the Enterprise Allowance Scheme. However, only one in twenty were known to have gone from Restart to training, and only one in two hundred into regular work, so the scheme can be judged to have had only a very limited initial impact.[40] YTS had been more successful in that, in the most recent evaluation, three out of five have gone into employment after the scheme. And while there were substitution effects, on balance YTS has induced extra jobs and recruitment.[41] Wider demographic and economic trends may be more successful than official training and employment policies in combating unemployment and 'welfare dependency'. Relevant in this context are the expected fall in the numbers of school-leavers during the next few years, together with the results of a more buoyant economy that, since 1986, has contributed to a downturn in the numbers of long-term unemployed.

Under workfare the dilemmas of participants, as well as those of government, become more acute, as our earlier discussion of American experience has also indicated. From a governmental perspective, the price of compulsion may well be a low provision of jobs by employers reluctant to take on forced labour, as well as opposition by trade unions. But failing to alter work-incentives through introducing an element of compulsion, changing the wage/benefit ratio, or inducing a greater adherence to the work ethic among some of those on the dole, reduces the credibility of the government's claims to be dealing with welfare dependency. From the participants' viewpoint there is the opportunity for training and employment that would not otherwise exist, and a consequent boost to present self-esteem and future prospects. But a number of features of these employment and training schemes remain problematic. Trainee status involves a loss of legal rights as employees, and the related failure to receive 'the rate for the job' may involve loss of self-confidence. The Low Pay Unit has warned that the young are being turned into an army of conscript labour.[42] Although YTS may be seen as part of an international trend to remove the under-eighteens from the labour market, the absence of choice in training, and the tendency for places to be concentrated in low-paid service and clerical work, mean that individuals' futures may be circumscribed.[43] Indeed, the Child Poverty Action Group has suggested that workfare places an 'obligation on recipients – without providing a way out of poverty'. It has quoted approvingly from an authoritative study of the USA model: 'workfare programmes did not create the work ethic, they found it'.[44]

The chicken-and-egg conundrum posed by unemployment and workfare is also evident in the interaction of social problems and consumerist policies advocated by government in the fields of housing, education and health. The shibboleths of tenant choice in housing, parental power in education or patient preference in health care, are not solutions to intractable difficulties but are themselves problematic. They raise complex issues concerning equity, information, finance and accountability.

In housing policy a main target for reform has been the management and control of four and a half million council houses. The emphasis in government pronouncements has been on the need to give tenants a choice of landlord, as in the Green Paper – 'Tenants' Choice' – of November 1987. But there are other, equally important, factors operating. The political dimension in housing – as has been argued for the post-war period – cannot be ignored; in this instance, the desire of a Conservative government to emasculate a mainly socialist, municipal monopoly over the public rented sector, and to replace it largely by a third sector of 'social housing' made up of cooperative and community ventures, housing associations and housing trusts. Also apparent is an attempt to lessen the 'culture of dependency' through the break-up of what is seen as a welfare ghetto; in 1987, two-thirds of households receiving supplementary benefits, half the long-term unemployed, and nearly three-fifths of single-parent families, lived on council estates.[45] Giving tenants the right to choose a new landlord – whether a Housing Association, the newly created Housing Action Trusts,[46] housing cooperatives or private landlords – is intended to change both the quality of management and the ethos of the estate. Just how poor council-housing management had become – as a result of financial stringency (imposed by central government) and the unresponsive nature of local housing bureaucracies – was revealed by the Audit Commission's Report of 1986 which found 85 per cent of council dwellings in need of repair and/or improvement.[47]

Parallel reforms are projected in the much smaller privately rented sector that are intended to reverse an accelerating long-run trend of declining provision, which has meant that even in the few years between 1979 and 1988 this sector had shrunk still further to just under 8 per cent of the housing stock.[48] The thrust of the policy must therefore be to make private rentals much more financially rewarding to private landlords. However, in line with the current emphasis on consumerism, it was tenant's choice that was emphasized in official pronouncements. 'De-regulation of private lettings is central to the government's policy of widening consumer choice in housing,' commented the Minister of Housing, William Waldegrave.[49]

[117]

The Housing Act of 1988 intends to end the policy of fair rents (begun in 1965) for new tenancies, and move to a system of 'market rents', but with some security of tenure given by 'assured tenancies'. These seem likely to give landlords increased powers to regain possession of property, and result in tenants having decreased ability to appeal successfully against higher rents. It is unlikely, however, that the measure will give the landlord sufficient incentive to reverse the very long-term decline in private letting.

The potential benefit to the economy in having a larger and more flexible rented-housing sector is obvious in facilitating greater mobility of labour. Mobility would help decrease unemployment levels through employing skills where they are needed. But the open-ended commitment to assist with higher market rents through housing benefit is causing Treasury concern. And the immediate economic and social implications of these housing reforms cause anxiety for both landlord and tenant. The Housing Associations fear the prospect of being squeezed between the more restricted benefits available to tenants and the higher rents that they should charge if in future they are to attract that 50 per cent of non-government money into private housing, which legislation has now deemed to be necessary. There are worrying economic implications for such associations in inheriting a back-log of repairs in ex-council housing, and more particularly when this is coupled with the management problems associated with the 'pepperpot' housing that will result from the patchy opting-out of tenants. For ex-council-house tenants, with a housing association or trust as their new landlord, there are problems of accountability; there is no longer the recourse to a vote in a local election as an expression of dissatisfaction over the housing record. And there are renewed fears of Rachmanism as rents rise to market levels. Government attempts to de-regulate the rented sector also worsen the plight of the poorest; on the subject of the steadily rising numbers of homeless people the Housing Act of 1988 remains resolutely silent. In further diminishing the stock of council housing, however, its provisions can only make it even more difficult for local councils to fulfil their legal obligation to provide the homeless with accommodation.

Diminishing social cohesion – arising from the increased differentiation that the legislation of the eighties encourages – is not just a feature of housing, but is also evident in the Education Reform Act of 1988. In educational provision this can only reinforce existing social inequalities, since pupils' performance at school will affect their later prospects as adults. Market principles are applied in the Act; the most conspicuous example being the 'opting-out' provision, whereby parents and governors of local authority schools may choose to become independent trusts. These are then funded directly by the Department of Education and Science as grant-maintained schools – revealingly termed 'independent state schools' by the Prime Minister. They may then select their pupils, although they must apply to the Secretary of State for Education before they can become grammar schools. Critics have seen this proposal as turning the educational clock back twenty years to the pre-comprehensive era, and have alleged that it will create privileged schooling for a minority. Increased variation will also result from the provision for open enrolment in all schools. The introduction of periodic, standard tests to all pupils in state schools is designed to enable parents to exercise consumer choice in the educational market place through a comparison of different schools' examination performance. The current practice of local education authorities (LEAs) placing ceilings on school numbers will end and allow schools to grow in response to parental demand. Reinforcing this increasing institutional autonomy will be the devolution of financial powers from LEAs to individual schools – which in future will control their own budgets.

Health reform is the fourth major item on the agenda of social reform in the late eighties and its discussion invokes the same principles of efficiency, accountability and consumer choice. But in health, as in education, the difficulty of consumers being in possession of sufficient information to make rational choices has not been given enough weight in reforming initiatives. The Health and Medicines Act seeks to make the Family Practitioner Service more competitive and responsive to patients by making government funding more closely geared to GPs' performance. And it extends hospital-style cash limits to what had been an open-ended system of financing in an attempt to spread scarce resources more efficiently. Reformers of the National Health Service have been concentrating on the need to increase the economic resources that the nation devotes to health care in the face of rising costs resulting from more sophisticated medical technology and the increased demands that are an inevitable result of an ageing population.[50] Confronting the dilemma of rising demand and finite resources is not new; options currently being debated to solve the funding crisis – including a health stamp and hospital charges – were rejected by the Conservative government in 1957, and again (as part of a more comprehensive review) by the Royal Commission on the National Health Service in 1979.[51] What are novel elements in the latest debates on the hospital service are the stresses on a greater 'cooperation' between the private and the public sectors, on the desirability of more resources being directed through the private sector in the provision of national health care, and on the more radical options under consideration for stimulating a more 'efficient' use of resources in the public sector.

International comparisons make clear that the UK devotes a smaller percentage of its GPD to health care than comparable European countries and much less than does the USA. Even more significant from the government's point of view is that the private sector is also much less important.[52] Currently only one in ten people are covered by private insurance in this country but the option of encouraging a greater take-up through tax relief on premiums has encountered Treasury resistance to giving a handout to over five million existing policy holders. Alternatives – giving individuals the right to opt out of a health stamp, or encouraging them to 'top up' a state health credit or voucher – are also on the political agenda for discussion. The concept of a state health credit that can be spent by the patient in either public or private facilities parallels the open enrolment scheme in education. In each case public money will follow the individual pupil or patient in their choice of the most efficient 'market' option, although it is not clear how the individual discerns this optimal choice. A more efficient use of resources within the NHS is also being considered through the device of internal markets where patients would travel across the boundaries of regional health authorities to areas with shorter waiting-lists.[53] And an aid to more efficient expenditure, as well as a means to increase the flow of private funds to the NHS, is already under way with a closer collaboration between private and public hospital facilities. This involves regional hospital administrators purchasing more cost-effective operations in private clinics for NHS patients waiting lengthy periods for treatment in public hospitals. Also at an early stage are cooperative deals between the public and private, which may involve jointly funded new facilities, or the building of private clinics beside NHS hospitals, which then purchase services from the NHS at commercially profitable rates.

Chronic under-funding of the hospital and community health service during the eighties has been of the order of £1.8 billion from 1980/1 to 1987–8, according to the all-party Social Services Committee. One result has been to alter the ideological climate within the NHS by forcing innovations that blur the private–public divide. This will make easier the implementation by a right-wing government of further radical policies previously seen as unacceptable to a public committed to a *national* health service. Yet the options must overcome grave difficulties. In practice, alternative methods of financing health care – notably through insurance – have proved much less effective elsewhere in restraining medical expenditure than has our own cash-limited NHS. And, in the face of a seemingly endless rise in demand, rationing of health care either by price or by queue seems inescapable. For example, the Health Maintenance Organizations (HMOs) in the USA that provide comprehensive health care in return for a fixed fee have attracted attention recently as a possible means to provide economical care for the growing number of elderly in this country. Under one proposal considered by the government, GPs would leave the NHS, taking their list of patients with them, together with a capitation fee for each of them, paid by government, but actuarially adjusted for age and therefore for likely health costs. The GPs would then be both insurers and providers of health care through forming free-standing HMOs that would provide total health care for patients. In order to provide both primary care and hospital care GPs would either contract with a hospital for services or possibly own one. Patients would be able to pay from their own pocket for additional costs.[54] In this scheme general practitioners would have a very direct interest – as they do not have at present – in keeping costs down. But this could lead to the drawbacks for patients that bedevil American HMOs. They suffer from the very same deficiencies that are seen as weaknesses in an overloaded NHS – queues, limited numbers of staff, and difficulty in getting access to specialist treatment. The attractions for government in expanding the private health care sector are, however, obvious.

The focus on inputs in current government thinking – with emphasis on the need for increased resources and enhanced efficiency – cannot postpone indefinitely the resolution of a more fundamental issue in the outputs of health care that are seen as desirable. Popular priorities may *not* be those of government, in which case it may have to face up to the implications of its consumerist rhetoric.

Popular Attitudes

Determining the nature of public attitudes towards welfare is a complex and increasingly politically contentious matter, but it is clearly important to have some sense of the popular views that will be one influence on the future direction of welfare reform. The inability of an overall verdict in a general election to give voters preferences on individual issues has contributed to the growth in opinion polls on topics such as welfare preference. But contrasting survey results – which may reflect the ideological persuasion of those who commission the polls – makes analysis problematic. Interpretation is further complicated by the need to evaluate the detailed format of questionnaires in any comparison; the use of varied language in different polls, for example, where questions about attitudes to 'needs' as against 'poverty' or 'welfare' may elicit different responses to the same basic question. The generality of questions in some early surveys has also led to the criticism that, for instance, asking individuals whether they would like better health provision, without ascertaining through more detailed queries whether they would also be prepared to pay more for improved provision, was a misleading exercise. The same line of argument suggests that, in future, market-type questions should find out about 'charitable' preferences for others in welfare services, as well as questions about one's 'own consumption' of welfare.

The results of surveys in *British Social Attitudes*, conducted annually from 1983 onwards, have indicated that there was broad support for the pre-1987/8 status quo in the welfare state.[55] The results of the 1987 survey were interesting in delineating a public opinion that would only partially give support to the kind of radical policy changes that were shortly to be implemented. Public support was particularly strong for the welfare heartland of pensions, health and education but there was some difference discernible between preference and payment, since those wishing to pay more for welfare provision and those wishing to preserve the status quo were about equal in number. Egalitarian sentiment was relatively weak; when the individual's pocket would suffer there was small support for redistributive income transfers through taxes and benefits. Significantly, in relation to the increasing emphasis on private welfare by the Thatcher ministries, there was tolerance for individuals to use their income to acquire improved provision; a majority of respondents were in favour of the affluent being allowed to pay for better health care, education, and pensions. But there appeared to be only minority support for more radically inegalitarian changes in the core provision of the welfare state as, for example, through transforming the NHS into a service used only by poorer individuals.

These surveys also showed that there was strong support for welfare benefits for the 'deserving' individuals – the sick, the old, the disabled – alongside a much lower level of approval for benefits to single-parent families, council-house tenants or the unemployed. One-third of respondents agreed that benefits were too high and discouraged people from finding jobs. Attitudes to these groups in the 1987 survey, as well as in the Medway Survey of the early eighties,[56] were a continuation of traditional attitudes to the 'undeserving'. Historically such discriminatory attitudes had been evident in popular moral interpretations of Victorian poverty, and in governmental concern over inter-war 'scrounging'. Media emphasis on the latter issue may also have reinforced popular prejudices during the twenties, as it was to do again later during the seventies.[57] However, a comparison of three surveys conducted from 1976 to 1987 suggests that there has been some weakening in moralistic and condemnatory attitudes by the British in their interpretation of causes of need.[58] While one might interpret this element in the surveys as suggesting some strengthening in the social solidarity felt by citizens of the welfare state, another finding undercut this by indicating that there was also an increasingly fatalistic attitude towards the inevitability of need.

Most surveys in recent years have been interpreted as showing widespread support for the welfare state. Since 1963, however, the Institute for Economic Affairs has conducted five surveys to find out whether demand for welfare has been matched by a public willingness to pay for it. In the absence of a market test of consumer preferences in welfare it has also attempted to find out 'suppressed public choice'. The IEA argues on the basis of its surveys that individuals' underlying choices challenge the alleged welfare consensus. If questions link services to cost there is a payment and preference split, with a change in response as questions move from general propositions on the desirability of extending or improving public welfare services, towards a focus on individual payment for them. Parallel to this, the IEA has found a substantial measure of support for contracting-out of state services in education and health, along the lines that have already been pioneered in pensions and housing.[59]

Results of surveys are convergent in suggesting a substantial but not unqualified support for public welfare. While core public services that benefit all classes receive substantial backing, there is much less sympathy for those deemed to be for a minority of undeserving recipients, and little enthusiasm for any further measures directed at a more egalitarian redistribution of resources in society. Interestingly, adherence to core public welfare services coexists with considerable support for private welfare options within a mixed economy of welfare. Unsatisfactory provision has also led to some consumer alienation, and hence to erosion of support for state welfare.[60] Relating these preferences to the radical welfare reforms of the third Thatcher government suggests that changes in social security, unemployment policy and council housing would be popular with the majority, that some of the educational reforms would receive a measure of support, but that current options being discussed for the NHS run contrary to a strong vein of popular support for existing patterns of health care.

That such a highly discriminatory set of public attitudes exists in the Britain of the late eighties indicates the limited character of the social consensus underpinning welfare. Popular assumptions about social expenditure, as well as the Thatcherite values informing welfare reform, have their roots in an individualistic British tradition. This has helped endow 'Victorian' virtues of thrift and self-reliance with current political appeal, and assisted in the justification of neo-liberal policies that will further increase social inequality. But the nineteenth-century 'social market', with its attendant economic inequalities, occurred in an undemocratic society, where political citizenship was limited by a restrictive property franchise. Today, the increasingly divided nature of our country – where significant numbers of people are in such poverty that it jeopardizes participation in the normal life of society – poses serious issues for democracy. The voice of Thatcherism argues that 'free enterprise if it is given the chance, is the least bad method yet invented to create for virtually all, jobs, prosperity, social and public services, and freedom'.[61] Yet even this vision of *embourgeoisement*, where choice grows through increased earnings, will leave some out in the cold. Early in 1988 there was a revealing indication of official concern over the lack of social cohesion in the government's appeal to the established church to preach the traditional virtues of deference and order so as to combat the results of social alienation in an increasingly crime-ridden and vandalized country. That such an appeal was thought to be necessary was itself an eloquent self-indictment of the socially divisive nature of Thatcherite policies.

VIII

Retrospect and Prospect

Debates in the late 1980s on the future of welfare have some striking parallels with those in the early 1830s which forced the change from the traditional, Elizabethan system of relieving the poor to the workhouse-dominated system of the Victorians. The Old Poor Law was then discredited as a welfare system out of control, by allegations of swollen poor rates, an inefficient bureaucracy, ever-increasing pauperism and – worst of all – an ensuing welfare dependency that harmed the economy.[1] The adoption of radical solutions in the New Poor Law had some immediate benefits, but the inadequate view taken of the need for social assistance by different groups, together with an incorrect analysis of the relationship between social policy and the economy, produced in the long run as many difficulties as had the earlier system. This is not to argue against the possibility of reform but to provoke awareness of likely limitations as well as anticipated advantages. An analysis of the relative merits and demerits of the welfare systems in our period will underline the point by suggesting some of the complexity of the social and economic balance sheet that past experience indicates should be considered, but which in practice is often precluded by narrow historical time horizons, economic pressure, or political expediency.

The workhouse system of the New Poor Law was a residual scheme in that it aimed to relieve destitution and not poverty. This was 'state welfare' at low cost and not the comparatively more expensive 'welfare state in miniature' of the Old Poor Law. To the Victorian poor its principal deficiencies were that this conditional and highly selective form of welfare conferred stigma along with minimal relief. The workhouse test of the New Poor Law effectively deterred the merely poor from applying for relief. Since the resulting costs of the *individual* poor were invisible because unquantifiable, and the reduced *social* costs in the form of lower poor rates were only too obvious, the reform was popular amongst the propertied classes. And not only was the system cheap but its supporters alleged that other social gains had been achieved in a greater self-reliance and enhanced thrift practised by the labouring poor. The claim that work-incentives were restored, and that after 1834 the feckless pauper of the Old Poor Law was transformed into an industrious worker, seems less plausible to the historian than it did to contemporaries. That an over-generous relief system had induced welfare dependency and voluntary unemployment was alleged at the time but, with the advantage of modern historical research, it is clear that this was mainly the result of rural under-employment arising from agrarian depression. If the poor-law system was implicated in the state of the economy, it was chiefly through high poor rates having increased employers' costs. But the overall lines of causation ran from the economy to the welfare system and not the other way round, a point that might usefully be borne in mind in relation to today's debates on welfare dependency and the unemployed.

Alongside the workhouse system were alternative forms of Victorian welfare. Indeed, these supplements – of informal care in the family, and voluntary care by charitable organizations – were present before, and after, the Poor Law. Familial care has traditionally been care both of first and last resort. For society, it is imbued with the moral virtue of self-help and has the additional asset of cheapness. For the individuals concerned it has the profound disadvantage that costs lie where they fall. Assumptions about its fundamental nature in a system of welfare have usually been unrealistic since they are predicated on a family structure that has never existed universally; with assumptions about female carers and male breadwinners, and of mutual dependency amongst members. An unevenness in provision is also a characteristic of the voluntary system; in practice this has always been less of a system than a patchwork of initiatives and improvisations. Today the voluntary agencies *may* possess advantages in flexibility, or in bringing in additional resources in the form of neighbourhood and community involvement. On the other hand, such voluntaryism also raises questions of acceptability in standards and of accountability in the use of funds donated or granted by the public. Current government thinking on restructuring welfare seems likely to place greater importance on the roles of informal care and of voluntary agencies. Too often in the recent past the planner's eye has been focused exclusively on the perceived need to restrict state welfare, and has failed to see the problems that this leads to in the alternatives. A more careful analysis of the real strengths and weaknesses of both familial and voluntary care would enable these to play an enhanced part in a spectrum of welfare agencies. But for them to do so requires a more sensitive facilitating role by the state in, for example, support services for home care, or of improved inspection of voluntary agencies in receipt of public funds. Paradoxically, using alternatives to public agencies more intensively may lead to a more – not less – complex involvement by the state in welfare provision.

Increasingly complex provision in response to greater than anticipated need had earlier been the experience of what had been intended to be a minimalist Victorian Poor Law. The reform of 1834 had concentrated on the 'able-bodied poor' because of labour-market considerations. In practice, administrators of relief found that these made up only a minority of applicants for relief, and that their work was largely concerned with 'helpless poor' – children, deserted and widowed women, the old and the sick. Also complicating their task still further were the vagrants, the feeble-minded, and the harmless insane. As a result, specialist provision for distinct categories of need grew up both inside and outside the Poor Law. By the early twentieth century the overlapping and unsystematized nature of social welfare had forced a fundamental rethinking of the state's role within a changing society. In its openness to radical options this Edwardian review was comparable to that in the 1980s. And the acceptance of the principle of social insurance was to set the agenda for social policy for the rest of the century. Yet the scope of this reform in 1911 was limited to those in stable employment, since funding depended on tripartite contributions from the state, the employee and the employer. This concentration on a sector of the labour force left out many, and gave a patriarchal bias to the insurance system that was to be retained in later developments. In ignoring the needs of many in the largest group in poverty – women – insurance-based welfare in the twentieth century compounded the omissions of the nineteenth-century Poor Law.

Insurance was a notable advance in welfare in providing *social* security and thus ensuring that risks did not lie where they fell but that the costs of misfortune were shared. Benefits as of right, in return for contributions, involved a new concept of social citizenship, as was emphasized by T. H. Marshall in his writings on social policy. These features were central to the extension of insurance into a national scheme after the Second World War. But these strengths involved corresponding weaknesses. Flat-rate contributions, low enough for even the poorly paid to afford, meant either restricted benefits or an erosion of the actuarial basis of insurance through hidden subsidy from general taxation. The scheme also assumed stable, high employment. The deficiencies within social insurance soon became apparent in the need to supplement insurance benefits by assistance, at first national assistance, then supplementary benefits, and now income support. A growing amount of such assistance was (and is) means-tested because this was seen as the most cost-effective way of providing selective help to those in greatest need.

The retreat from universality to selectivity in a growing range of welfare payments has been the central feature of the last forty years. Universality in provision met the ideal of social citizenship and thus avoided stigmatizing minority recipients of welfare, but the cost of providing all benefits to every citizen has increasingly been seen in Britain as so prohibitively costly as to be unrealistic. Selectivity was advocated on grounds of cost, and because it was thought to target resources where need was greatest. Once selectivity had been in operation for some time its disadvantages became apparent. Individuals were confronted with a system so complex that few could understand their entitlements, while resulting low rates of take-up of means-tested benefits was affected by the stigma that some still felt was attached to selective benefits. The state found problems in identifying groups in need and had to shoulder high administrative costs in operating an increasingly complicated set of regulations. Public anxiety about eroded work-incentives, because of high benefit/wage ratios, proved difficult to remove in the face of the continuing poverty traps (or poverty plateaux) experienced by low-income families.

Targeting resources through selectivity has led to concern about a two-tier welfare state. But welfare is already highly divisible once the fiscal and occupational welfare states are brought into the analysis. Advocates of these fiscal and occupational systems argue that they possess a number of advantages: they can reduce some of the deficiencies brought about by flat-rate national insurance contributions and low rates of state benefit (as in private occupational pension schemes); or they may increase the resources available (as with private health insurance). And such consumer-orientated welfare enables the citizen to exercise a greater degree of individual responsibility in his chosen welfare mix. Welfare consumerism is therefore often aligned with the 'Victorian' virtues of self-reliance and the just reaping of (unequal) rewards for differentiated effort. This is then contrasted unfavourably with a state system that breeds 'welfare dependency' amongst the poor who receive selectively targeted benefits. That the benefits of the fiscal and occupational systems are themselves targeted – but to different social groups – may be overlooked. So too may a parallel but hidden form of 'dependency' (in the form of mortgage relief) by the relatively affluent.

Not only is there much differentiation between private and public welfare but within the public welfare sector there is very variable provision for similar situations. A good example is provision for the unemployed, where the long-term unemployed are much less generously treated than those without jobs for a short period. In many respects this merely repeats the welfare inadequacies of the twenties and thirties. Just as high inter-war unemployment led to a series of *ad hoc* expedients which discriminated against those out of work for substantial periods, so there has been a failure in the eighties to compensate for the economic consequences of long-term unemployment in adequate welfare benefits. This also underlines another drawback to Britain's possession of one of the most highly selective benefit systems in Europe: unenlightened self-interest can reduce the citizen's willingness to pay for others' welfare benefits. In this situation, moral hazard and welfare dependency are always the characteristics of others.

The ideological nature of the New Right's attack on the welfare state has been accompanied by a disregard of empirical data. Yet both historical and contemporary evidence suggests some difficulty in simplifying the role of an advanced capitalistic state in welfare provision for its citizens. Rolling back the frontiers of the welfare state may well involve a redrawing of the boundaries between market and non-market provision but may increase – rather than reduce – their interlocking complexity. The inspiration that Victorian models have provided for neo-liberal thinking on social policy during the eighties also appears likely to further develop our highly divisible welfare system along historical lines. The growth of means-testing has already eroded the citizen's 'right' to benefit, and thereby stigmatized the claimant. Workfare-style policies have repeated the conditionality of benefits that was characteristic of the workhouse system. How far we are prepared to go along this road is uncertain. But that we have travelled a considerable distance was suggested by the conclusions of an authoritative study of urban deprivation in 1985: 'A growing number of people are excluded by poverty or powerlessness from sharing in the life of our nation. A substantial minority . . . are forced to live on the margins of poverty or below the threshold of an acceptable standard of living.'[2] Setting the requirements of humanity in social welfare policies against those of efficiency in the market involves striking a balance between social and economic markets in our mixed economy. That the scales are tipping decisively against humanity is indicated by recent discussion of the desirability of workfare policies by politicians on the political right. One such statement predicted that workfare 'will come to the advanced [*sic*] societies. If the unemployed say we want to opt out . . . don't expect us to pay you to do nothing.'[3] That individuals 'chose' unemployment would seem a familiar moral judgement to those who designed the workhouses of the New Poor Law 150 years ago to serve as a corrective for people who 'chose' poverty.

Notes

I. Introduction

1 R. Matthews, C. Feinstein, J. Odling Smee, *British Economic Growth, 1856–1973* (1984), p. 498.

2 D. Donnison, *The Politics of Poverty* (1982), p. 226.

3 A. Seldon, 'The Idea of the Welfare State and its Consequences', in S. N. Eisenstadt and O. Ahimeir, eds., *The Welfare State and its Aftermath* (Totowa, New Jersey, 1985), p. 61.

4 P. Johnson, 'Some Historical Dimensions of the Welfare State "Crisis" ', *Journal of Social Policy*, 15 (1986), pp. 443, 459, 463.

5 A. Peacock, *The Welfare Society* (Liberal Party publication, 1961).

6 I. Gough, 'Thatcherism and the Welfare State', *Marxism Today* (July 1980), p. 8.

7 Mr Henry McLeish, MP for Fife Central, in *Hansard*, vol. 127, no. 91, p. 419.

8 See A. Weale, 'Ideology and Welfare', *Quarterly Journal of Social Affairs*, 2 (1986), pp. 197–219 and A. Weale, *Political Theory and Social Policy* (1983), chapters 1, 2, 5, for an illuminating discussion of these complex issues.

9 A. Briggs, 'The Welfare State in Historical Perspective', *European Journal of Sociology*, 2 (1961).

II. Comparative Perspectives

1 OECD, *The Welfare State in Crisis* (Paris, 1981).

2 OECD, *Social Expenditure, 1960–1990* (Paris, 1985).

3 J. Higgins, 'Comparative Social Policy', *Quarterly Journal of Social Affairs*, 2 (1986), pp. 221–42.

4 A. J. Heidenheimer, H. Heclo, C. T. Adams, *Comparative Public Policy. The Politics of Social Choice in Europe and America* (1976), p. 257.

5 For a useful introduction to this categorization, see D. E. Ashford, *The Emergence of the Welfare States* (Oxford, 1986), pp. 20–9; T. Skocpol,

'Bringing the State Back In: Strategies of Analysis in Current Research', in P. B. Evans, D. Rueschemeyer, and T. Skocpol, eds., *Bringing the State Back In* (Cambridge, 1985), pp. 3–37.

6 G. V. Rimlinger, *Welfare Policy and Industrialization in Europe, America and Russia* (1971), p. 35.

7 Sven Aspling, quoted in D. Jenkins, *Sweden: the Progress Machine* (1968), p. 68.

8 J. Burton, *Would Workfare Work?* (Employment Centre, University of Buckingham, 1987), pp. 18–23.

9 R. Erikson and R. Åberg, *Welfare in Transition. A Survey of Living Conditions in Sweden, 1968–1981* (Oxford, 1987), chapter 14.

10 H. M. Hermes, 'Women and the Welfare State: the Transition from Private to Public Dependence', in Sassoon, ed., *Women and the State* (1987), p. 85; A. Borchast and B. Siim, 'Women and the Advanced Welfare State', in Sassoon, ed., *Women and the State*, pp. 128–9, 153.

11 P. Meyerson, *The Welfare State in Crisis – the Case of Sweden* (Federation of Swedish Industries, Stockholm, 1982), p. 21.

12 S. Larsson and K. Sjöström, 'The Welfare Myth in Class Society', in J. A. Fry, ed., *Limits of the Welfare State. Critical Views on Post-war Sweden* (1979), pp. 169, 187; R. Huntford, *The New Totalitarians* (1971), pp. 183, 198.

13 J. Hartmann, 'Social Policy in Sweden (1950–1980)', in R. Girod, P. de Laubier and A. Gladstone, eds. *Social Policy in W. Europe and the USA, 1950–1980, An Assessment* (1985), p. 97.

14 Meyerson, *The Welfare State in Crisis*, p. 49.

15 R. Erikson, 'Has Swedish Welfare Experience Led to Passivity and Dependency?' Unpublished paper given at Nuffield College, University of Oxford, in February 1988.

16 *Economist*, 21 November 1987.

17 M. B. Katz, *Poverty and Policy in American History* (New York, 1983), pp. 239–41; S. Mencher, *Poor Law to Poverty Program* (Pittsburgh, 1967), pp. 254–5.

18 F. F. Piven and R. A. Cloward, *Regulating the Poor. The Functions of Public Welfare* (1972), p. 198.

19 J. T. Patterson, *America's Struggle against Poverty, 1900–1980* (Cambridge, Mass., 1981), pp. 134, 180–1.

20 *The Times*, 1 August 1854. Quoted in C. Leman, *The Collapse of Welfare Reform: Political Institutions, Policy and the Poor in Canada and the United States* (Cambridge, Mass., 1980), p. 1.

21 In 1959/60 there were 7.1 million on welfare and 22 per cent of the population in poverty, compared to a situation in 1973/4, where the comparable figures were 14.4 million and 11 per cent. In the international league table of welfare spending as a percentage of GDP, the USA

moved from twentieth to seventeenth from the mid-sixties to 1974. (Patterson, *America's Struggle*, pp. 166, 171).

22 Quoted in P. Beneton, 'Trends in the Social Policy Aims of the United States (1960–80)', in R. Girod, *et al.* eds., *Social Policy in W. Europe and the USA 1950–1980. An Assessment* (1985), p. 77.

23 *Made in the USA. A review of Workfare: the compulsory work-for-benefits regime* (Unemployment Unit, 1987), pp. 5–8.

24 T. J. Addison, 'A Synopsis of "Workfare": the United States Experience', in Burton, *Would Workfare Work?*, pp. 57–9.

25 See the helpful discussion of the inaccuracy of this term as applied to AFDC recipients, in Patterson, *America's Struggle*, pp. 201–2.

26 L. Burghes, 'Does Workfare Work?', *Poverty*, 68 (1987/8), pp. 9–10.

27 *New York Times*, 2 February 1987.

28 R. Hanson, 'The Expansion and Contraction of the American Welfare State', in R. E. Goodin and J. le Grand, eds., *Not Only the Poor* (1987), p. 181; *New York Times*, 12 April 1987; *San Francisco Chronicle*, 22 June 1987.

29 *New York Times*, 23 March 1987.

30 C. Murray, *Losing Ground. America's Social Policy 1950–1970* (New York, 1984), p. 229. See also L. Mead, *Beyond Entitlement: the Social Obligations of Citizenship* (1986) for a comparable view.

31 G. T. Burtless and R. H. Haveman, *Taxes, Transfers and Economic Distortions: Evaluating the New View* (Brookings Institution, Washington, 1987); S. Danziger and D. Weinberg, eds., *Fighting Poverty. What Works and What Doesn't* (Cambridge, Mass., 1987); W. Wilson, *The Truly Disadvantaged: the Inner City, the Underclass and Public Policy* (Chicago, 1987).

32 K. G. Banting, *Poverty, Politics and Policy. Britain in the 1960s* (1979), chapter 4, *passim*; J. Higgins, *The Poverty Business in Britain and America* (Oxford, 1978).

33 P. Ruggles and M. O'Higgins, 'Retrenchment and the New Right: A Comparative Analysis of the Impacts of the Thatcher and Reagan Administrations', in M. Rein, G. Esping-Andersen, L. Rainwater, eds., *Stagnation and Renewal in Social Policy. The Rise and Fall Of Policy Regimes* (Armonk, New York, 1987), pp. 160–90.

34 H. Laming, *Lessons from America: the Balance of Services in Social Care* (Policy Studies Institute Discussion Paper 11, 1985).

35 The main American insurance-based programmes are: Old Age, Survivors, Disability Insurance; Unemployment Insurance; Workmens' Compensation; Medicare. The main assistance programmes are: Supplemental Security Income; AFDC; General Assistance; Food Stamps; Medicaid; and Health Care for Indigents.

36 Goodin and le Grand, eds., *Not Only the Poor*, pp. 165, 192–3.

37 Heidenheimer *et al.*, *Comparative Public Policy*, pp. 258–9.
38 H. Heclo, *Modern Social Politics in Britain and Sweden. From Relief to Income Maintenance* (New Haven, 1974), pp. 320–2.
39 Paper by Prof. Walter Korpi to a conference on 'The Goals of Social Policy: Past and Future' held at the London School of Economics, December 1987.
40 Ruggles and O'Higgins, 'Retrenchment', p. 165.
41 Heidenheimer *et al.*, *Comparative Public Policy*, p. 280.
42 *Social Expenditure*, p. 62.

III. Victorian and Edwardian Welfare Policies

1 The New Poor Law did not apply to Scotland, where the Poor Law was re-organized in 1845, when a central Board of Supervisors was set up to oversee the parochial local boards.
2 D. C. Marsh, *The Welfare State* (1970), p. 22.
3 A. Digby, *The Poor Law in Nineteenth-century England and Wales* (Historical Association, 1982), pp. 9–13.
4 J. D. Marshall, *The Old Poor Law 1795–1834* (second edn., 1985), pp. 16–17. (The comments are those of R. H. Tawney and M. Blaug.)
5 M. A. Crowther, *The Workhouse System 1834–1929* (1981), p. 14.
6 Quoted in C. F. Bahmueller, *The National Charity Company. Jeremy Bentham's Silent Revolution* (Berkeley, 1981), p. 207.
7 K. Williams, *From Pauperism to Poverty* (1981), pp. 85–9; M. E. Rose, 'The Allowance System under the Poor Law', *Economic History Review*, second series, XIX (1966), pp. 607–20; A. Digby, *Pauper Palaces* (1978), pp. 105–14.
8 See the helpful discussion in P. Spicker, *Stigma and Social Welfare* (1984), pp. 3–19.
9 *Report of the Royal Commission on the Poor Laws and Relief of Distress, 1909, Majority Report*, part VI, p. 544.
10 O. MacDonagh, 'The Nineteenth-century Revolution in Government: A Reappraisal', *Historical Journal*, 1 (1958); D. Roberts, *Victorian Origins of the British Welfare State* (1960).
11 M. Carpenter, *Reformatory Schools for the Children of the Perishing and Dangerous Classes, and for Juvenile Offenders* (1851), p. 2.
12 A. Fried and R. Elman, eds., *Charles Booth's London* (Harmondsworth, 1971), pp. 54–8.
13 B. S. Rowntree and B. Lasker, *Unemployment. A Social Study* (1911), chapter 5, *passim*; W. H. Beveridge, *Unemployment. A Problem of Industry* (2nd edn., 1930), pp. 133–7.
14 For a useful discussion of this complex concept of the underclass during

the inter-war period, see J. Macnicol, 'In Pursuit of the Underclass', *Journal of Social Policy*, 16 (1987), pp. 293–318.

15 A. Deacon and J. Bradshaw, *Reserved for the Poor. The Means Test in British Social Policy* (1983), pp. 179–80.

16 H. Land, 'The Introduction of Family Allowances: An Act of Historic Justice?', in P. Hall, H. Land, and R. Parker, eds., *Change, Choice, and Conflict in Social Theory* (1975).

17 H. Perkin, 'Ideology and the Roots of Welfare', paper given at SSRC Conference on 'The Roots of Welfare', Lancaster University, December 1983; A. J. Taylor, *Laissez-faire and State Intervention in Nineteenth-century Britain* (1972), pp. 48–9; E. J. Evans, ed., *Social Policy 1830–1914. Individualism, Collectivism and the Origins of the Welfare State* (1978), p. 5.

18 *Leeds Mercury*, 29 March 1844.

19 *Hansard*, third series, CCXXC, col. 525.

20 R. Lambert, *Sir John Simon 1816–1904*, p. 370.

21 B. B. Gilbert, *The Evolution of National Insurance in Great Britain. The Origins of the Welfare State* (1966), p. 15.

22 H. Pelling, *Popular Politics and Society in Late Victorian Britain* (1977), p. 4; P. Thane, 'The Working Class and State "Welfare" in Britain, 1880–1914', *Historical Journal*, 27 (1984), p. 899.

23 E. P. Hennock, 'Poverty and Social Theory in England: the Experience of the Eighteen Eighties', *Social History*, I (1976), p. 91.

24 G. Himmelfarb, 'The Idea of Poverty', *History Today*, 4 (1984), p. 28.

25 B. Semmel, *Imperialism and Social Reform* (1960), p. 16; A. Offer, 'Empire and Social Reform: British Overseas Investment and Domestic Politics, 1908–14', *Historical Journal*, 26 (1983), pp. 137–8.

26 E. P. Hennock, *British Social Reform and German Precedents. The Case of Social Insurance, 1880–1914* (Oxford, 1987), p. 209.

27 *Manchester Guardian*, 17 January 1895.

28 E. P. Hennock, 'The Origins of British National Insurance and the German Precedent' in W. J. Mommsen, ed., *The Emergence of the Welfare State in Britain and Germany* (1981), p. 84.

29 J. Harris, *William Beveridge. A Biography* (Oxford, 1977), pp. 170–7.

30 R. Hay, 'Employers and Social Policy in Britain: the Evolution of Welfare Legislation, 1905–1914', *Social History*, 4 (1977), pp. 435–55.

31 *The Times*, 19 June 1889.

32 Quoted in P. Thane, 'Non-contributory versus Insurance Pensions, 1878–1908', in P. Thane, ed., *The Origins of British Social Policy* (1978), p. 98.

33 Quoted in D. Fraser, *The Evolution of the British Welfare State* (second edn., 1984), p. 172.

34 *Hansard*, 29 April 1909.

35 Hennock, *British Social Reform*, p. 210.
36 *The Times*, 12 June 1911.

IV. The Emergence of the Classic Welfare State

1 A. Deacon, *In Search of the Scrounger: The Administration of Unemployment Insurance in Britain 1920–1931* (1976); A. Deacon and J. Bradshaw, *Reserved for the Poor. The Means Test in British Social Policy* (Oxford, 1983), chapter 5.
2 T. Prosser, 'The Politics of Discretion: Aspects of Discretionary Power in the Supplementary Benefits Scheme', in M. Adler and S. Asquith, eds., *Discretion and Welfare* (1981), pp. 154–5.
3 A. Peacock and J. Wiseman, *The Growth of Public Expenditure in the United Kingdom* (second edn., 1967), p. 91.
4 M. Bruce, *The Coming of the Welfare State* (fourth edn., 1968), p. 290.
5 B. B. Gilbert, *British Social Policy, 1914–1939* (New York, 1970), p. vii.
6 R. M. Titmuss, *Problems of Social Policy* (1950).
7 S. Andrzejewski, *Military Organization and Society* (1954).
8 *The Times*, 28 February 1940.
9 P. Abrams, 'The Failure of Social Reform, 1918–20', *Past and Present*, 24 (1963).
10 R. Lowe, 'The Erosion of State Intervention in Britain, 1917–24', *Economic History Review*, XXXI (1978).
11 Deacon, *In Search of the Scrounger*, p. 9.
12 M. A. Crowther, 'Family Responsibility and State Responsibility in Britain before the Welfare State', *Historical Journal*, 25 (1982), p. 139.
13 For contrasting interpretations, see C. Webster, 'Health, Welfare and Unemployment During the Depression', *Past and Present*, 106 (1985), pp. 204–30; and J. M. Winter, 'Unemployment, Nutrition and Infant Mortality in Britain, 1920–50', in J. M. Winter, ed., *The Working Class in Modern Britain* (Cambridge, 1983), pp. 233–56.
14 Political and Economic Planning, *Report on the British Social Services* (1937), p. 12.
15 H. Pelling, *The Labour Governments, 1945–51* (1984), pp. 117–18.
16 *Our Towns. A Close-Up* (second edn., Oxford, 1944), p. xiii (the comment was that of the Women's Group on Public Welfare); J. Macnicol, 'The Effect of the Evacuation of Schoolchildren on Official Attitudes to State Intervention', in H. Smith, ed., *War and Social Change. British Society in the Second World War* (Manchester, 1986), p. 27.
17 1 July 1940.
18 4 January 1941.
19 *Social Insurance and Allied Services. Report by Sir William Beveridge* (Command Paper 6404, HMSO, 1942), p. 172.

20 18 December 1942.

21 K. Jefferys, 'British Politics and Social Policy during the Second World War', *Historical Journal*, 30 (1987), pp. 124, 132, 137.

22 *Social Insurance*, p. 17.

23 J. Harris, *William Beveridge. A Biography* (Oxford, 1977), p. 360.

24 'Family Allowances and Less Eligibility', in P. Thane, ed., *The Origins of British Social Policy* (1978), p. 173.

25 The quotation from Butler's diary is given in Jefferys, 'British Politics', p. 140.

26 A. K. Cairncross, *Years of Recovery. British Economic Policy, 1945–51* (1985), pp. 457–61.

27 R. C. O. Matthews, 'Why has Britain had Full Employment since the War?', *Economic Journal*, 78 (1968), pp. 555–69.

28 W. H. Beveridge, *Full Employment in a Free Society* (1960), p. 199.

29 M. Foot, *Aneurin Bevan. A Biography* (2 vols., 1973), pp. 11, 105.

30 C. Webster, *The Health Services since the War. Volume 1. Problems of Health Care. The National Health Service before 1957* (HMSO, 1988), p. 80. I am most grateful to the author for allowing me to read this before publication.

31 Ibid, p. 82.

32 J. Harris, 'Did British Workers Want the Welfare State? G. D. H. Cole's Survey of 1942', in Winter, *The Working Class*, p. 203.

33 K. Harris, *Attlee* (1982), p. 281.

34 *Social Insurance*, p. 130.

35 *Hansard*, 6 February 1946, 418, col. 1751.

36 *Hansard*, 4 July 1948, 444, col. 1631.

37 D. Rubinstein, 'Socialism and the Labour Party: the Labour Left and Domestic Policy, 1945–1950', in D. E. Martin and D. Rubinstein, eds., *Ideology and the Labour Movement* (1979), pp. 226–8.

38 J. Saville, 'The Welfare State: An Historical Approach', in E. Butterworth and R. Holman, eds., *Social Welfare in Modern Britain* (1975), p. 64.

39 J. Lewis, 'Dealing with Dependency: State Practices and Social Realities, 1870–1945', in J. Lewis, ed., *Women's Welfare. Women's Rights* (1983); G. Pascall, *Social Policy. A Feminist Analysis* (1986), chapter 7 *passim*; P. Thane, 'Women and the Poor Law in Victorian and Edwardian England', *History Workshop*, 6 (1978); H. Land, 'The Family Wage', *Feminist Review*, 6 (1980).

40 K. O. Morgan, *Labour in Power* (Oxford, 1984), p. 142.

V. Forty Years on from Beveridge

1 *The Times*, 25 January 1984.

2 A. Deacon, 'Was There a Welfare Consensus? Social policy in the 1940s',

in C. Jones and J. Stevenson, eds., *The Yearbook of Social Policy in Britain, 1983* (1984), pp. 25–38.

3 *Social Insurance and Allied Services. Report by Sir William Beveridge* (Command Paper 6404, 1942), para. 302.

4 Ibid, para. 307.

5 Ibid, para. 305.

6 Ibid, para. 308.

7 Ibid, para. 27.

8 A. B. Atkinson, *Poverty in Britain and the Reform of Social Security* (Occasional Paper 18 of Department of Applied Economics, Cambridge, 1969), p. 24.

9 *Social Insurance*, para. 23.

10 A. B. Atkinson, A. K. Maynard, and C. G. Trinder, 'National Assistance and Low Incomes in 1950', *Social Policy and Administration* (1981), pp. 19–31.

11 A. B. Atkinson, *The Economics of Inequality* (second edn., 1983), p. 269.

12 A. Deacon and J. Bradshaw, *Reserved for the Poor*, pp. 1, 98.

13 *The Times*, 17 January 1952.

14 *Report of the Ministry of Social Security* (1966), p. 50.

15 Atkinson, *The Economics of Inequality*, p. 270.

16 J. Bradshaw, 'Tried and Found Wanting: The Take-up of Means-tested Benefits' in S. Ward, ed., *DHSS in Crisis. Social Security Under Pressure and Under Review* (Child Poverty Action Group, 1985), pp. 103–4.

17 *The Structure of Personal Income, Taxation, and Income Support* (the Meacher Report), (1983), para. 1.4.

18 J. Bradshaw and A. Deacon, 'Social Security', in P. Wilding, ed., *In Defence of the Welfare State* (Manchester, 1986), pp. 89–90.

19 M. Brown and N. Madge, *Despite the Welfare State* (DHSS/SSRC, 1982), p. 286.

20 9 and 10 GEO. 6 c 81.

21 *Report of the Royal Commission on the National Health Service* (Command Paper 7615, HMSO, 1979), para. 2.6.

22 A. Digby and N. Bosanquet, 'Doctors and Patients in an Era of National Health Insurance and Private Practice', in *Economic History Review*, second series, XLI (1988).

23 P. Townshend and N. Davidson, eds., *Inequalities in Health. The Black Report* (Harmondsworth, 1982), pp. 66–75, 206.

24 *Independent*, 26 January 1988.

25 M. J. Daunton, *A Property-owning Democracy? Housing in Britain* (1987), pp. 62–4.

26 A. Murie, 'Housing', in Wilding, *In Defence of the Welfare State*, p. 68.

27 *Financial Times*, 23 May 1987.

VI. Other States of Welfare

1 R. Titmuss, *Commitment to Welfare* (2nd edn., 1976), p. 53.

2 W. H. Beveridge, *Voluntary Action: A Report on Methods of Social Advance* (1949), pp. 301–2.

3 T. H. Marshall, *Social Policy in the Twentieth Century* (1970), p. 184.

4 K. Gregson, 'Poor Law and Organized Charity: The Relief of Exceptional Distress in the North-east of England, 1870–1919', in M. E. Rose, ed., *The Poor and the City: the English poor law in its urban context* (Leicester, 1985), p. 96.

5 F. Prochaska, *Women and Philanthropy in 19th Century England* (Oxford, 1980), p. 110.

6 B. Harrison, 'Philanthropy and the Victorians', *Victorian Studies*, IX (1966).

7 From 1988 SERPS was modified (in order to cut the cost of the scheme in the twenty-first century), with pensions based on 20 per cent not 25 per cent of earnings, and on average lifetime earnings not the best twenty years, as at present. Private occupational schemes are expected to provide proportionately more of future pensions.

8 P. Thane, 'Non-contributory versus Insurance Pensions, 1878–1908', in P. Thane, ed., *The Origins of British Social Policy* (1978), p. 88.

9 *Guardian*, 19 February 1983; see also the speeches by M. Thatcher and K. Baker on this theme reported in the *Guardian* of 28 April 1988.

10 R. M. Kramer, *Voluntary Agencies in the Welfare State* (Berkeley, 1981), pp. 283–4; R. M. Kramer, 'The Welfare State and the Voluntary Sector: The Case of the Personal Social Services', in S. N. Eisenstadt and O. Ahimeir, eds., *The Welfare State and its Aftermath* (Totowa, New Jersey, 1985), pp. 137–40.

11 M. Thatcher, 'Facing the New Challenge', in C. Ungerson, ed., *Women and Social Policy. A Reader* (1985), pp. 214–15. This speech was given on 19 January 1981 to the Women's Royal Voluntary Service.

12 G. Pascall, *Social Policy. A Feminist Analysis* (1986), p. 101.

13 H. Rose, 'Re-reading Titmuss: The Sexual Division of Welfare', *Journal of Social Policy*, 10 (1981), pp. 493–4.

14 Pascall, *Social Policy*, p. 102.

15 P. Thane, 'Women and the Poor Law in Victorian and Edwardian England', *History Workshop*, 6 (1978), pp. 36–7.

16 M. A. Crowther, 'Family Responsibility and State Responsibility in Britain before the Welfare State', in *Historical Journal*, 25 (1982), p. 132.

17 J. Lewis, *The Politics of Motherhood. Child and Maternal Welfare in England, 1900–1939* (1980), p. 18.

18 O. Banks, *Faces of Feminism. A Study of Feminism as a Social Movement* (Oxford, 1981), p. 176.

19 J. Lewis, 'Eleanor Rathbone 1872–1946', in P. Barker, ed., *Founders of the Welfare State* (1984), p. 89.

20 Equal Opportunities Commission, *Caring for the Elderly and Handicapped: Community Care Policies and Women's Lives* (Manchester, 1982), p. 31; I. Webb, *People Who Care – A Report on Carer Provision in England and Wales* (Co-operative Women's Guild, 1988).

21 J. Finch and D. Groves, 'Community Care and the Family: A Case for Equal Opportunities?', in Ungerson, *Women and Social Policy*, p. 219.

22 DHSS, *Growing Older* (1981), para. 1.11.

23 Titmuss, *Commitment to Welfare*, p. 104.

24 R. M. Titmuss, *Essays on The Welfare State* (third edn., 1976), pp. 41–2, 44–5.

25 *Housing Policy: a Consultative Document* (Department of the Environment, 1977), p. 49.

26 Titmuss, *Essays*, pp. 50–1.

27 F. Field, *Inequality in Britain. Freedom, Welfare and the State* (1981).

28 For a useful recent discussion see P. Spicker, 'Titmuss's "Social Division of Welfare": A Reappraisal', in C. Jones and J. Stevenson, eds., *The Yearbook of Social Policy in Britain, 1983* (1984), pp. 182–93.

29 P. Taylor-Gooby, *Public Opinion, Ideology and State Welfare* (1985), pp. 84–5.

30 L. Hannah, *Inventing Retirement. The Development of Occupational Pensions in Britain* (Cambridge, 1986), pp. 45, 51, 115, 125.

31 J. Higgins, 'Private Medicine: The Changing Scene', in M. Brenton and C. Ungerson, eds., *The Yearbook of Social Policy in Britain, 1986–7* (1987), pp. 101, 105, 111; *Independent*, 27 May 1987.

32 Taylor-Gooby, *Public Opinion*, p. 64.

33 J. le Grand, *The Strategy of Equality. Redistribution and the Social Services* (1982), p. 137; R. E. Goodin and J. le Grand, eds., *Not Only the Poor* (1987), p. 204.

34 For further reading on this point see J. Dale, 'Feminists and the Development of the Welfare State – Some Lessons from our History', *Critical Social Policy*, 16 (1986), pp. 57–65; M. David and H. Land, 'Sex and Social Policy', in H. Glennerster, ed., *The Future of the Welfare State. Remaking Social Policy* (1983), pp. 138–56; H. Land, 'Women and Children Last: Reform of Social Security?' in M. Brenton and C. Ungerson, eds., *The Yearbook of Social Policy in Britain, 1985–6* (1986), pp. 24–41; H. Land, 'Women: Supporters or Supported?', in D. L. Barker and S. Allen, eds., *Sexual Division and Society. Process and Change* (1976), pp. 108–32; H. Land, 'The Family Wage', *Feminist Review*, 6 (1980); G. Pascall, 'Women and Social Welfare', in P. Bean and S. Macpherson, eds., *Approaches to Welfare* (1983), pp. 83–98.

VII. Views from the Eighties

1 In the autumn of 1987 and spring of 1988, Kenneth Baker (Secretary of State for Education) visited city science schools, John Moore (Minister of Health and Social Security) studied libertarian ideas on welfare, and Norman Fowler (Minister of Labour) looked at the Boston Compact, a voluntary partnership between schools and industry which gives school-children priority in getting local jobs.

2 Article by W. Rees Mogg in *Independent*, 1 February 1988.

3 'The Welfare State: Breaking the Post-War Consensus', *Political Quarterly*, 51 (1980), p. 17.

4 'Political Ideas and the Debate on State Welfare, 1940–45', in H. L. Smith, ed., *War and Social Change. British Society and the Second World War* (Manchester, 1986), pp. 248–9.

5 W. H. Beveridge, *Power and Influence* (1953), pp. 360–1.

6 E. Heath, J. E. Powell, I. McLeod, R. Carr, *One Nation* (1950), p. 9.

7 I. McLeod and J. E. Powell, *The Social Services: Needs and Means* (Conservative Political Centre, 1952), p. 5.

8 T. H. Marshall, 'The Welfare State: A Comparative Study', in *Sociology at the Crossroads* (1963); D. Wedderburn, 'Facts and Theories of the Welfare State', in R. Milliband and J. Saville, eds., *The Socialist Register 1965*, pp. 143–4.

9 R. Klein, 'The Welfare State: A Self-Inflicted Crisis', *Political Quarterly*, 51 (1980), p. 29.

10 R. Bacon and W. Eltis, *Britain's Economic Problem: Too Few Producers* (1976).

11 Sir Keith Joseph, *Reversing the Trend – a Critical Re-appraisal of Conservative Economic and Social Policies* (1975), p. 7.

12 *Independent*, 10 October 1987.

13 *Social Trends 18* (HMSO, 1988), p. 112; *Economic Trends* (January 1988).

14 *Social Trends 18*, pp. 65, 83, 97, 132, 134–5.

15 *Social Trends 18*, p. 135; *Economic Trends* (November 1987); *Occupational Mortality, The Registrar General Decennial Supplement for Great Britain, 1879–80 to 1982–3* (1986); *Guardian*, 30 July 1986.

16 Speech to the Conservative Conference in October 1987 re-using words formerly in the Labour Electoral Manifesto of October 1974 (*Independent*, 10 October 1987).

17 Ibid.

18 *Independent*, 10 and 11 October 1987.

19 *Sunday Times*, 28 September 1987.

20 The workhouse test was self-acting in that the deterrent conditions in the house (including wearing a prison-like uniform, separation from other members of your family, and boring routines including compulsory

work) meant that only the really destitute – as distinct from the merely poor – would enter and so receive poor relief.

21 T. Skocpol, 'America's Incomplete Welfare State: The Limits of the New Deal Reforms and the Origins of the Present Crisis', in M. Rein, G. Esping-Andersen, L. Rainwater, eds., *Stagnation and Renewal in Social Policy. The Rise and Fall of Policy Regimes* (New York, 1987), p. 53.

22 *Sunday Times*, 20 March 1988.

23 *Independent*, 13 November 1987.

24 *Hansard*, vol. 121, no. 30, p. 180. (Examples of benefit cuts have been that earnings-related unemployment pay was ended in 1982 and pensions have been raised in line with prices rather than earnings.)

25 Ibid.

26 The budget in the first year of operation is £200 million; this is £150 million less than was recommended by the Social Security Advisory Committee. This body also advocated that only 30 per cent should be in the form of loans, as against 70 per cent in the Act.

27 *Hansard*, vol. 121, no. 30, p. 180.

28 *Training for Employment* (Command Paper 316 HMSO, 1988)

29 *Guardian*, 23 February 1988. Job Clubs help those unemployed for over six months by providing advice and facilities to find jobs.

30 *Guardian*, 7 April 1988, reporting the Sixth Report of the Social Security Advisory Committee. Under the Social Security Act of 1975 there had been a disqualification from benefit of 13 weeks, and this became 26 weeks under the 1988 Social Security Act. Those eligible for supplementary benefit – or income support – will have a 40 per cent reduction over the longer period.

31 Expenditure on Swedish training schemes averages £13,000 per head, and the more successful schemes in the USA over £10,000, compared to only £5,000 in the UK (*Guardian*, 22 February 1988).

32 Lord Young, as reported in *Poverty*, 68 (1987/8); Norman Fowler, reported in *Hansard*, vol. 127, no. 91, p. 415.

33 Letter to the *Guardian*, 25 February 1988, by the Opposition Spokesperson on Employment, Clare Short; statements by Michael Meacher on Fowler's lack of credibility in *Hansard*, vol. 127, no. 91, p. 443.

34 *Economist*, 28 November 1987.

35 *Independent*, 3 November 1988.

36 N. Fowler in *Hansard*, vol. 127, no. 91, p. 415.

37 JTS was introduced in 1987 but there was a shortfall in places offered, the scheme was weakened by trade-union opposition, and characterized by low take-up and high drop-out rates.

38 The scheme began in 1982. In attempting to occupy those aged 25 or more who had been out of work for more than a year, it succeeded

mainly in providing largely menial work, with minimal training to facilitate later entry to the labour market.

39 Paper to the Manpower Services Commission of January 1988, reported in the *Independent*, 7 January 1988.

40 Manpower Services Commission, 87/24, Annex 1, Table 3.

41 *Unemployment Bulletin* (25 December 1987), p. 6; B. M. Deakin and C. F. Pratten, 'Economic Effects of YTS', *Employment Gazette* (October 1987), pp. 491–3.

42 *Independent*, 24 October 1988.

43 'Workfare and the Duty to Train', unpublished paper given at Nuffield College, Oxford, in February 1988 by Kate Laydon (Director of Youth Aid).

44 L. Burghes, 'Does Workfare Work?' *Poverty*, 68 (1987/8), p. 11. The American study cited is J. M. Gueron, *Work Initiatives for Welfare Recipients*, Manpower Demonstration Research Corporation (March 1986), p. 14.

45 *Financial Times*, 23 May 1987.

46 Housing Action Trusts are government-funded bodies which are to get £125 million from 1988 to 1991 in order to revitalize run-down estates in inner-city areas, before transferring them to private landlords or back to councils.

47 *Managing the Crisis in Council Housing* (HMSO, 1986).

48 *Hansard*, vol. 123, no. 54, p. 620.

49 'Application of Economic Logic to Clarify the Housing Market', in the *Independent*, 22 January 1988.

50 In 1986 there were one and a half times the number of over 65s that there were in the opening years of the NHS. And whereas one in five are over 60 in the mid-eighties, there will be one in four by 2025, while numbers over 85 will double in the same period. Health care costs increase dramatically with age. Comparing those in the UK for 15 to 64 year olds, those for 65 to 74 year olds are twice as high, and those aged 75 or over, eight times as high. (P. S. Heller *et al.*, *Aging and Social Expenditure in the Major Industrial Countries, 1980–2025*. Occasional Paper 47, IMF, 1988, p. 37.)

51 *Financial Times*, 1 January 1988 (reporting on cabinet discussions disclosed by the opening of manuscripts in the Public Record Office under the 30-Year Rule); *Royal Commission on the Health Service*, (Command Paper 7615, HMSO, 1979), chapter 21 *passim*.

52 In 1984 the UK devoted 5.9 per cent of GDP on health care compared to Germany with 8.1 per cent, France with 9.1 per cent, and the USA with 10.7 per cent. Private spending in the UK made up only 0.6 per cent, compared to Germany with 1.7 per cent, France 2.6 per cent, and the

USA with 6.3 per cent (OECD, *Financing and Delivering Health Care*, Paris, 1987).

53 The idea was that of A. N. Enthoven, in *Reflections on the Management of the NHS* (Nuffield Provincial Hospitals Trust, 1985).

54 *The Times*, 23 February 1988.

55 P. Taylor-Gooby, 'Citizenship and Welfare', in R. Jowell, S. Witherspoon, L. Brook, eds., *British Social Attitudes, the 1987 Report* (1987), pp. 1–28.

56 P. Taylor-Gooby, *Public Opinion, Ideology, and State Welfare* (1985), p. 43.

57 P. Golding and S. Middleton, *Images of Welfare. Press and Public Attitudes to Poverty* (Oxford, 1982).

58 R. Jowell *et al.*, *British Social Attitudes 1987*, p. 10.

59 R. Harris and A. Seldon, *Welfare Without the State. A Quarter-century of Suppressed Public Choice* (1987), p. 51.

60 P. Taylor-Gooby, 'Welfare Attitudes: Cleavage, Consensus and Citizenship', *Quarterly Journal of Social Affairs*, 3 (1987), pp. 203, 205.

61 Maiden speech by Lord Joseph of Portsoken in the House of Lords (*Independent*, 20 February 1988).

VIII. Retrospect and Prospect

1 S. G. and E. O. A. Checkland, eds., *The Poor Law Report of 1834* (Harmondsworth, 1974), pp. 128, 145, 167, 182.

2 *Faith in the City. A Call for Action by Church and Nation. The Report of the Archbishop of Canterbury's Commission on Urban Priority Areas* (1985), p. 359.

3 Michael Heseltine, reported in the *Financial Times*, 5 March 1988.

Select Bibliography

General

Briggs, A., 'The Welfare State in Historical Perspective', *European Journal of Sociology*, 2, 1961
Eisenstadt, S. N., and Ahimeir, O., eds., *The Welfare States and its Aftermath*, Totowa, New Jersey, 1985
Gilbert, N., *Capitalism and the Welfare State. Dilemmas of Social Benevolence*, New Haven, 1983
Gough, I., *The Political Economy of the Welfare State*, London, 1979
Johnson, P., 'Some Historical Dimensions of the Welfare State "Crisis" ', *Journal of Social Policy*, 15, 1986
Mishra, R., *The Welfare State in Crisis. Social Thought and Social Change*, New York, 1984
OECD, *The Welfare State in Crisis*, Paris, 1981
Offe, C., *Contradictions of the Welfare State*, London, 1984
Pascall, G., *Social Policy. A Feminist Analysis*, London, 1986
Weale, A., 'Ideology and Welfare', *Quarterly Journal of Social Affairs*, 2, 1986
—, *Political Theory and Social Policy*, London, 1983

Comparative Welfare

General
Ashford, D. E., *The Emergence of the Welfare State*, Oxford, 1986
Evans, P., Rueschemeyer, D., and Skocpol, T., eds., *Bringing the State Back In*, Cambridge, 1985
Flora, P., and Heidenheimer, A. J., eds., *The Development of Welfare States in Europe and America*, London, 1981
Heidenheimer, A. J., Heclo, H., and Adams, C. T., *Comparative Public Policy. The Politics of Social Choice in Europe and America*, London, 1976
Heller, P. S., Hemming, R., and Kohnert, P. W., *Aging and Social Expenditure in the Major Industrial Countries, 1980–2025*, IMF Occasional Paper 47, 1988

Higgins, J., *States of Welfare. Comparative Analysis in Social Policy*, Oxford, 1981

—, 'Comparative Social Policy', *Quarterly Journal of Social Affairs*, 2, 1986

Mommsen, W. J., ed., *The Emergence of the Welfare State in Britain and Germany*, London, 1981

OECD, *Social Expenditure, 1960–1990*, Paris, 1985

Rein, M., Esping-Andersen, G., and Rainwater, L., eds., *Stagnation and Renewal in Social Policy. The Rise and Fall of Policy Regimes*, New York, 1987

Rimlinger, G. V., *Welfare Policy and Industrialization in Europe, America and Russia*, London, 1971

Sassoon, A. Showstack, ed., *Women and the State: The Shifting Boundaries of Public and Private*, London, 1987

Specific Countries
USA

Hanson, R. L., 'The Expansion and Contraction of the American Welfare State', in Goodin, R. E., and le Grand, J., eds., *Not Only the Poor. The Middle Classes and the Welfare State*, London, 1987

Made in the USA. A Review of Workfare: The Compulsory Work-for-benefits Regime, Unemployment Unit, 1987

Mencher, S., *Poor Law to Poverty Program*, Pittsburgh, 1967

Murray, C., *Losing Ground. American Social Policy 1950–1980*, New York, 1984

Patterson, J. T., *America's Struggle against Poverty, 1900–1980*, Cambridge, Mass., 1981

Piven, F. F., and Cloward, R. A., *Regulating the Poor. The Functions of Public Welfare*, London, 1972

Sweden

Erikson, R., and Åberg, R., *Welfare in Transition. A Survey of Living Conditions in Sweden, 1968–1981*, Oxford, 1987

Hartmann, J., 'Social Policy in Sweden (1950–1980)', in Girod, R., de Laubier, P., and Gladstone, A., eds., *Social Policy in W. Europe and the USA, 1950–1980. An Assessment*, London, 1985

Heclo, H., *Modern Social Politics in Britain and Sweden. From Relief to Income Maintenance*, New Haven, 1974

Rosenthal, A. H., *The Social Programs of Sweden*, Minneapolis, 1967

Victorian and Edwardian Britain

Checkland, S. G. and E. O. A., eds., *The Poor Law Report of 1834*, Harmondsworth, 1974

Crowther, M. A., 'The Later Years of the Workhouse 1890–1929', in Thane, P., ed., *The Origins of British Social Policy*, London, 1978

Digby, A., *The Poor Law in Nineteenth-century England and Wales*, Historical Association, 1982

Evans, E. J., ed., *Social Policy 1830–1914. Individualism, Collectivism and the Origins of the Welfare State*, London, 1978

Fraser, D., *The Evolution of the British Welfare State*, second edn., London, 1984

—, ed., *The New Poor Law in the Nineteenth Century*, London, 1976

Gilbert, B. B., *The Evolution of National Insurance in Great Britain. The Origins of the Welfare State*, London, 1966

Hay, R., 'Employers and Social Policy in Britain: The Evolution of Welfare Legislation', *Social History*, 4, 1977

—, *The Origins of the Liberal Welfare Reforms, 1906–1914*, London, 1975

Hennock, E. P., *British Social Reform and German Precedents. The Case of Social Insurance, 1880–1914*, Oxford, 1987

Himmelfarb, G., 'The Idea of Poverty', *History Today*, 4, 1984

Pelling, H., *Popular Politics and Society in Late Victorian Britain*, London, 1977

Roberts, D., *Victorian Origins of the British Welfare State*, New Haven, 1960

Rose, M. E., *The Relief of Poverty 1834–1914*, second edn., 1986

Semmel, B., *Imperialism and Social Reform*, London, 1960

Taylor, A. J., *Laissez-faire and State Intervention in Nineteenth-century Britain*, London, 1972

Thane, P., 'Non-contributory versus Insurance Pensions, 1878–1908', in Thane, P., ed., *The Origins of British Social Policy*, London, 1978

Thane, P., 'The Working Class and State "Welfare" in Britain, 1880–1914', *Historical Journal*, 27, 1984

Thane, P., 'Women and the Poor Law in Victorian and Edwardian England', *History Workshop*, 6, 1978

Britain from 1914 to 1951

Abrams, P., 'The Failure of Social Reform, 1918–20', *Past and Present*, 24, 1963

Addison, P., *The Road to 1945. British Politics and the Second World War*, London, 1975

Beveridge, W. H., *Social Insurance and Allied Services. Report by Sir William Beveridge*, Command Paper 6404, HMSO, 1942

—, *Full Employment in a Free Society*, London, 1944

Booth, A., 'The "Keynesian Revolution" in Economic Policy Making', *Economic History Review*, second series, XXXVI, 1983

Crowther, M. A., 'Family Responsibility and State Responsibility in Britain before the Welfare State', *Historical Journal*, 25, 1982

—, *Social Policy in Britain, 1914–39*, London, 1988

Deacon, A., *In Search of the Scrounger: The Administration of Unemployment Insurance in Britain 1920–1931*, London, 1976

—, 'Was there a Welfare Consensus? Social Policy in the 1940s', in Jones, C., and Stevenson, J., eds., *The Yearbook of Social Policy in Britain, 1983*, London, 1984

Digby, A., and Bosanquet, N., 'Doctors and Patients in an Era of National Health Insurance and Private Practice, 1913–1939', *Economic History Review*, second series, XLI, 1988

Gilbert, B. B., *British Social Policy, 1914–1939*, New York, 1970

Glynn, S., and Booth, A., eds., *The Road to Full Employment*, London, 1987

Harris, J., *William Beveridge. A Biography*, Oxford, 1977

Harris, J., 'Political Ideas and the debate on State Welfare, 1940–45', in Smith, H., ed., *War and Social Change. British Society in the Second World War*, Manchester, 1987

Jefferys, K., 'British Politics and Social Policy during the Second World War', *Historical Journal*, 30, 1987

Land, H., 'The Family Wage', *Feminist Review*, 6, 1980

Lewis, J., *The Politics of Motherhood. Child and Maternal Welfare in England, 1900–1939*, London, 1980

—, 'Dealing with Dependency: State Practices and Social Realities, 1870–1945', in J. Lewis, ed., *Women's Welfare. Women's Rights*, London, 1983

Lowe, R., 'The Erosion of State Intervention in Britain, 1917–24', *Economic History Review*, second series, XXXI, 1978

Macnicol, J., 'Family Allowances and Less Eligibility', in Thane, P., ed., *The Origins of British Social Policy*, London, 1978

Macnicol, J., 'In Pursuit of the Underclass', *Journal of Social Policy*, 16, 1987

Macnicol, J., 'The Effect of the Evacuation of Schoolchildren on Official Attitudes to State Intervention', in Smith, H., ed., *War and Social Change. British Society in the Second World War*, Manchester, 1986

Peden, G. C., 'Sir Richard Hopkins and the "Keynesian Revolution" in Employment Policy, 1929–45', *Economic History Review*, second series, XXXVI, 1983

Rubinstein, D., 'Socialism and the Labour Party: the Labour Left and Domestic Policy, 1945–1950', in Martin, D. E., and Rubinstein, D., eds., *Ideology and the Labour Movement*, London, 1979

Webster, C., 'Healthy or Hungry Thirties?', *History Workshop Journal*, 10, 1982

—, 'Health, Welfare and Unemployment During the Depression', *Past and Present*, 106, 1985

—, *The Health Services since the War. Volume 1. Problems of Health Care. The National Health Service before 1957*, HMSO, 1988

Whiteside N., 'Counting the Cost: Sickness and Disability among Working

People in an Era of Industrial Recession', *Economic History Review*, second series, XL, 1987

Winter, J. M., *The Great War and the British People*, London, 1985

—, ed., *The Working Class in Modern Britain*, Cambridge, 1983

Britain after 1951

Abel-Smith, B., 'The Welfare State: Breaking the Post-War Consensus,' *Political Quarterly*, 51, 1980

Atkinson, A. B., *The Economics of Inequality*, second edn., London, 1983

Brown, M., ed., *The Structure of Disadvantage*, London, 1983

—, and Madge, N., *Despite the Welfare State*, DHSS/SSRC, 1982

Burton, J., *Would Workfare Work?*, Employment Centre, University of Buckingham, 1987

Deacon, A., and Bradshaw, J., *Reserved for the Poor. The Means Test in British Social Policy*, Oxford, 1983

Donnison, D., *The Politics of Poverty*, Oxford, 1982

Glennerster, H., *Paying for Welfare*, Oxford, 1985

Golding, P., and Middleton, S., *Images of Welfare. Press and Public Attitudes to Poverty*, Oxford, 1982

Goodin, R. E., and le Grand, J., *Not Only the Poor. The Middle Classes and the Welfare State*, London, 1987

Gough, I., 'Thatcherism and the Welfare State', *Marxism Today*, July 1980

Green, D. G., *The New Right. The Counter-Revolution in Political, Economic and Social Thought*, Brighton, 1987

Hall, P., Land, H., Parker, R., and Webb, A., *Change, Choice and Conflict in Social Policy*, London, 1975

Halsey, A. H., ed., *Trends in British Society since 1900. A Guide to the Changing Social Structure of Britain*, second edn., London, 1988

Harris, R., and Seldon, A., *Welfare Without the State. A Quarter-century of Suppressed Public Choice*, London, 1987

Land, H., 'Women and Children Last: Reform of Social Security?', in Brenton, M., and Ungerson, C., eds., *The Yearbook of Social Policy in Britain 1985–6*, London, 1986

Marquand, D., 'Beyond Social Democracy', *Political Quarterly*, 58, 1987

Marshall, T. H., *Social Policy in the Twentieth Century*, London, 1970

—, 'Citizenship and Social Class', in *Sociology at the Crossroads*, London, 1963

Pascall, G., 'Women and Social Welfare', in Bean, P., and Macpherson, S., eds., *Approaches to Welfare*, London, 1983

Ruggles, P., and O'Higgins, M., 'Retrenchment and the New Right: A Comparative Analysis of the Impacts of the Thatcher and Reagan Administrations', in Rein, M., Esping-Andersen, G., and Rainwater, L., eds.,

Separation and Renewal in Social Policy. The Rise and Fall of Policy Regimes, London, 1987

Saville, J., 'The Welfare State: An Historical Approach', *New Reasoner*, 1957/8

Report of the Royal Commission on the Health Service, Command Paper 7615, HMSO, 1979

Taylor-Gooby, P., 'Welfare Attitudes: Cleavage, Consensus and Citizenship', *Quarterly Journal of Social Affairs*, 3, 1987

Townshend, P., *Poverty in the UK. A Survey of Household Resources and Standards of Living*, Harmondsworth, 1979

—, and Bosanquet, N., eds., *Labour and Inequality*, London, 1972

—, and Davidson, N., eds., *Inequalities in Health. The Black Report*, Harmondsworth, 1982

Ward, S., ed., *DHSS in Crisis. Social Security Under Pressure and Under Review*, Child Poverty Action Group, London, 1985

Wedderburn, D., 'Facts and Theories in the Welfare State', in Milliband, R., and Saville, J., eds., *The Socialist Register 1965*, London, 1965

Wilding, P., ed., *In Defence of the Welfare State*, Manchester, 1986

Other Welfare States

Finch, J., and Groves, D., 'Community Care and the Family: A Case for Equal Opportunities?' in Ungerson, C., ed., *Women and Social Policy. A Reader*, London, 1985

Harrison, B., 'Philanthropy and the Victorians', *Victorian Studies*, IX, 1966

Hannah, L., *Inventing Retirement. The Development of Occupational Pensions in Britain*, Cambridge, 1986

Higgins, J., 'Private Medicine: The Changing Scene', in Brenton, M., and Ungerson, C., eds., *The Yearbook of Social Policy in Britain, 1986–7*, London, 1987

Kramer, R. M., *Voluntary Agencies in the Welfare State*, Berkeley, 1981

Spicker, P., 'Titmuss's "Social Division of Welfare": A Reappraisal', in Jones, C., and Stevenson, J., eds., *The Yearbook of Social Policy in Britain, 1983*, London, 1984

Titmuss, R. M., 'Community Care: Fact or Fiction', in *Commitment to Welfare*, second edn., 1976

—, 'The Social Division of Welfare', in *Essays on the Welfare State*, third edn., 1976

Webb, I., *People Who Care – A Report on Carer Provision in England and Wales*, Co-operative Women's Guild, 1988

Wolfenden Committee, *The Future of Voluntary Organizations*, London, 1978

Index